# TUMTUM AND NUTMEG: TROUBLE AT ROSE COTTAGE

# TUMTUM AND NUTMEG: TROUBLE AT ROSE COTTAGE

## Emily Bearn

### *Illustrated by Nick Price*

First published 2010
by Egmont UK Limited
This Large Print edition published by
AudioGO Ltd
by arrangement with
Egmont Books 2012

ISBN: 978 1445 883205

British Library Cataloguing in Publication Data available

Printed and bound in Great Britain by
MPG Books Group Limited

*For Brian*

# Chapter One

It was quite a mystery. There was Nutmeg, rootling around in the Mildews' larder, all alone with her shopping basket swung over her arm—when suddenly she heard a voice speaking to her very sharply.

'Put that back!' it said as she plucked a raisin from the fruitcake. 'Put that back or I shall call the police!'

Nutmeg jumped, dropping her raisin in fright. She knew it wasn't a human voice she had heard—it had been much too small for that. It sounded like a mouse. But who could it be?

She looked up and down the larder shelves, peering along the tins and boxes. But there was no sign of anyone at all.

*I must have been imagining things, she thought. After all, who would want to call the police over a raisin? I've been borrowing raisins from this larder for as long as I can remember, and no one's*

1

*ever complained about it before.*

She picked the raisin up again, to show that she wasn't really frightened at all. But just as she was lifting it into her basket, the little voice piped up again: 'Thief! Thief! I'll report you to Chief Constable Watchmouse!'

Nutmeg gulped. She knew she wasn't imagining things now, for the voice was very clear.

'Who are you?' she asked nervously. 'Why don't you come out?'

There was no reply.

'Oh, do let me see you!' she pleaded. But now the little voice had gone quite silent. Nutmeg did not like it at all. 'Now look here,' she said, trying to sound firm. 'You've no right to tell me what to do. My name is Mrs Nutmouse, and I live at Nutmouse Hall, and my husband and I have been borrowing crumbs and raisins and sugar lumps from this larder ever since—'

But then all of a sudden there was a great explosion of giggles, echoing all around the larder. 'Tee! He! Tee! He! Tee! He! *Hissssssss!*'

Nutmeg could be in no doubt now

3

that it was a mouse, for mice giggle quite unlike any other creatures do. And it sounded as if there were two of them!

'Oh, do stop it!' she said tearfully. 'Please come out, whoever you are!'

But the giggling got louder and louder, until Nutmeg simply couldn't bear it a moment longer. She hurtled for the door, with her paws pressed to her ears; and as she ran out of the larder, another voice, deeper than the first, rang after her: 'Off you go, shoo! And don't come back in our larder!'

By the time Nutmeg got back to Nutmouse Hall, she was in a terrible state.

'Tumtum!' she cried, bursting into the kitchen.

Tumtum looked up in alarm from his crumpet. 'Whatever's happened?' he asked.

'Oh, Tumtum, it was simply awful!' Nutmeg sobbed. 'They were laughing at me, and poking fun at me, and saying they'd call the police and report me for borrowing a raisin from the fruit cake! But it was only a stale old fruit

4

cake, and I know Mr Mildew wouldn't mind and, and . . .'

'*Who* said they would call the police?' Tumtum asked in astonishment. 'Was it Arthur and Lucy? Did they see you?'

'Oh, no, no, not them!' Nutmeg sobbed. 'They're still at school. It was mice—horrid, teasing mice! And they told me it was *their* larder, and that I should never come back!'

'*Their* larder!' Tumtum spluttered. 'I trust you informed them that my family has been living at Rose Cottage for the last—'

'Yes, yes,' Nutmeg interrupted. 'I tried to explain, but they just kept on laughing at me.'

Tumtum was furious. 'Who were they?' he asked. 'Louts from the village I expect. What did they look like? Did you get their names?'

'Oh, but that's the worst thing about it,' Nutmeg said miserably. 'I didn't even see them. They didn't come out! They must have been watching me from behind a jar or a cake tin—the larder's full of places to hide. And the way they called it *their* larder makes me think they might have moved in!'

'*Moved in*!' Tumtum said fearfully. 'Are you sure?'

'Well, it's possible,' Nutmeg said. 'You should have heard the way they were talking—they sounded as if they owned the place.'

Tumtum looked very alarmed. He didn't want any other mice moving into Rose Cottage. It wouldn't do at all.

He stood up and pulled on his jacket.

'I'll go and have a word with them,' he said. 'I'll tell them the Nutmouses are the only mice who've ever lived at Rose Cottage since the mouse history books began. They'll just have to move on somewhere else.'

'Oh, do be careful, dear!' Nutmeg pleaded. 'They sounded horrid!'

'Don't you worry,' Tumtum replied, giving her paw a squeeze. 'They're probably just a pair of silly school mice having a bit of fun.'

Nutmeg waited anxiously in Nutmouse Hall while Tumtum crept out into the Mildews' kitchen.

He tiptoed round the larder door,

6

and peered nervously inside. But there was no sign of anything unusual. Everything was quite still.

'Hello!' he called out awkwardly. 'Is anybody there? It's Mr Nutmouse here, from Nutmouse Hall.'

No reply.

'Hello, there,' Tumtum called again. 'Now listen here. You've no right to talk to my wife like that. Come out, I say! Come out and let me see you!'

But there was not a sound. Tumtum wondered if Nutmeg had been imagining things. She had been up late last night, potting and pickling her autumn fruits, and her mind might have been playing tricks on her.

*She's probably just tired*, he thought. And he was about to turn back, when suddenly he heard a strange noise:

*Buzzzzzzzz! Grrrrrrrrrr!*

Tumtum froze. What could it be? It sounded like an engine, or a huge bee. And it seemed to be coming from above him—but when he looked up there was nothing there.

The noise was only faint at first, but then it got louder and louder, until it

was throbbing all around him.

There was a blasting wind that battered his clothes, and when Tumtum turned round he saw the most astonishing sight. It was Arthur's toy helicopter, taking off from the top shelf!

Tumtum watched in amazement as the helicopter crashed over a biscuit tin and roared into the air. He thought it was going to fly out into the kitchen. But then all at once it dipped its nose and dived towards him!

Tumtum gave a yelp of terror. He tried to run, but he was blinded by a sudden cloud of flour, and the roar of the engine was so loud he felt his ears would burst.

'Help!' he cried. '*HELP!*'

He tried to duck behind the flour bin, but the gust from the propellers knocked him flat on his back. He lay helpless on the floor, trembling with fear.

And as the helicopter barrelled over above him, he saw two mice snarling down at him from the cockpit. They were both snow white—and they had gold fangs.

# Chapter Two

Tumtum had never seen a mouse with gold fangs before, and for a moment he felt he was dreaming. *I'll wake up soon, and it will all be over*, he thought hopefully.

But then he saw the helicopter looping round the larder, and thundering back towards him—and he knew it wasn't a dream at all. It was quite real. He ran for the door, but the helicopter swooped after him, flying so low it made his ears flap.

Then the cockpit window slid open, and one of the mice leaned out. 'BOMBS AHOY!' he yelled, hurling down a peanut.

Tumtum dived out of the way just in time, and as he looked up he saw the helicopter roaring into the kitchen.

Tumtum felt very shaken. But he wanted to see where the mice had gone. The helicopter they were flying in belonged to Arthur. He hadn't had it long, and it was his favourite toy. Tumtum knew he'd want it back.

Slowly, he staggered to his feet, and peeked round the larder door. He saw the helicopter buzz down to land on the table, then the cockpit door opened and the two mice clambered out. They were wearing black suits, and they had the same white fur and fang-like gold teeth. But in other ways they were very different.

One was as thin as a toothpick, while the other was round and squishy, like a ball of dough.

The thin mouse glided on to the table without a sound, but the fat one was heavy and short of breath. He huffed and panted, and his nose kept twitching, as if he were hunting for food.

Tumtum thought they both looked most unusual. *They must be town mice, dressed like that, he thought curiously. Whatever are they doing at Rose Cottage?*

Then the fat mouse suddenly gave a high-pitched squeal: 'Food! Food!' And

he started waddling across the table.

'Oi! Snout! Where are you going?' the thin mouse barked.

'Food! Food!' Snout squeaked, pointing to a plate at the far end of the table. It contained a bit of ham sandwich left over from Mr Mildew's lunch. He hurried over to it, then clambered up and started guzzling noisily.

The thin mouse followed. But he took only one sniff, then turned away in disgust.

'Revolting,' he snarled, in a voice so cold it made Tumtum shiver. 'This whole place is filthy. It's not fit for a flea! No wonder no other mice live here—except those two doddery old fools we saw in the larder.'

'Well they won't bother us again after the fright we gave them,' Snout replied, wiping a blob of mustard from his lips.

He finished the sandwich with a belch. 'I'm still hungry, Dad,' he whined, scouring round the kitchen for something else to eat. Then: 'Look!' he cried, pointing excitedly at the dresser.

'Let's fly over there and steal those chocolates!'

He was pointing to a large box of caramel creams, which Uncle Jeremy had given to Arthur and Lucy when he came to stay. The children were not often given chocolates, so they were being careful to make them last. So far, they had only eaten two each.

Tumtum watched helplessly as the two mice clambered back into the helicopter, and flew over to the dresser. They landed just beside the chocolate box. Then they slithered out, and loaded every single caramel cream inside. It was quite a big helicopter, and there was just enough room for all the chocolates in the hatch.

Tumtum was horrified. What would the children think when they came home to find all their chocolates gone? He did not dare let the mice see him again, for he knew he would be no match for them on his own. But he was determined to find out where they were hiding.

He watched as they jumped back into the cockpit, and circled into

14

the air.

*Vrrrrooooooom! Grrrrrrrrrr!*

The helicopter roared over the kitchen table, and round the vegetable rack, then it turned and started flying towards the sink.

Tumtum gulped. One of the glass panes in the window above the sink was missing, leaving a hole just big enough for the toy helicopter to pass through. And for a moment, Tumtum feared the mice were going to escape outside—then Arthur would never get his helicopter back. But instead, the helicopter started to hover downwards, until it was almost touching the floor. Then it turned, and swished through the little gingham curtain hanging under the sink.

Tumtum gazed after it, feeling very puzzled. There was nothing under the sink except for some old cloths and detergent bottles. Surely the mice couldn't be hiding in there? Tumtum was very curious. So he decided to creep after them, and find out what was going on.

He went up to the sink on tiptoe,

15

and cautiously poked his nose under the curtain.

It was pitch black, and at first he couldn't see a thing. But then suddenly a light came on, and how Tumtum stared!

The light was coming from a big bleach bottle at the back of the cupboard. It had a door and two windows cut out of it, and the words scrawled in big black letters on the front.

GOLDFANG TOWER property of
Mr GOLDFANG and his son SNOUT
KEEP OUT

The helicopter was parked beside the bleach bottle, and Goldfang and his son were busy unloading the chocolates, and carrying them inside.

The bleach bottle was well lit. Tumtum supposed it must be where the mice were staying. But what an odd place to choose! While their backs were turned, he wriggled out

16

BLEACH

GOLDFANG TOWER
property of
Mr GOLDFANG and
his son SNOUT
KEEP
OUT

from under the curtain and crept a little closer, until he could just see in through the windows. The mice had made a staircase out of a scrubbing brush, and arranged themselves on two floors. And to Tumtum's surprise, the rooms looked well furnished, with pretty curtains and chairs, and beds and a chintz sofa. There was even a piano.

Tumtum frowned, for somehow the furniture all looked very familiar. He peered through the windows, trying to think where he had seen it before. Then suddenly he remembered.

'Good grief!' he whispered. *'They've burgled the doll's house!'*

# Chapter Three

Tumtum was very shocked.

And when he returned to Nutmouse Hall and told Nutmeg all that had happened, she looked at him in amazement.

'They . . . they . . . *bombed you with a peanut?*' she stammered, trying to take it all in.

Tumtum nodded. 'And you should have seen inside their bleach bottle,' he said. 'It was full of things stolen from the doll's house. They've taken the beds and the chairs and the grand piano—they've even stolen those pretty gingham curtains you made last year!'

Nutmeg was horrified. 'And you say they had gold teeth?'

'That's right,' Tumtum said. 'Long and sharp, just like daggers. Goldfang and Snout are their names—they're father and son. And they've called their home Goldfang Tower!'

'But I just don't understand it,'

19

Nutmeg said. 'They must be town mice if they're wearing black suits. No country mouse would dress like that. But why would they want to come and stay in Rose Cottage? There are no shops or restaurants here, or any of the other things town mice like. And the Mildews' larder is always bare. They'd find much better pickings in the Manor House.'

Tumtum nodded. He couldn't understand it either. 'I reckon they're up to something,' he said. 'I just wish I knew what it was.'

'Well, whatever it is, they can jolly well get up to it somewhere else!' Nutmeg said firmly. 'We can't have mice who behave like that living at Rose Cottage!'

Tumtum agreed. But he didn't dare go and tell the Goldfangs to leave, for he knew they would do something very nasty to him if he did.

'We shall have to report them to Chief Constable Watchmouse,' he said. 'If we tell him that two town mice have broken into Rose Cottage, and stolen a helicopter and burgled a doll's house, then he'll come and arrest them at once.'

'But don't you remember, dear, the Chief Constable's on his annual break,' Nutmeg said. 'He's gone slug-spotting in Merrydown Meadow, and he won't be back for a whole week.'

Tumtum sighed. A week is a long time in a mouse's life. And the Chief Constable was a very keen slug-spotter—if he saw a particularly exotic slug, he might forget himself, and stay away even longer.

But then Tumtum had another idea. 'Why don't we ask Arthur and Lucy to catch the Goldfangs for us,' he said. 'We can write them a letter, telling them where they are hiding, then they can take them by surprise.'

Nutmeg was delighted with this plan. 'Oh, what fun!' she said. 'Just think what a fright the Goldfangs will get when they see the children peering into their bleach bottle!'

So Tumtum found a piece of paper, and Nutmeg wrote the children a letter, explaining everything.

She wanted to deliver it to the attic

at once, so they would find it when they came home from school. But she was too late. For it was already four o'clock, and just as she was sealing the envelope, a door slammed in Rose Cottage, making the whole of Nutmouse Hall shake. Then they heard Arthur and Lucy crashing into the kitchen.

'Blow!' Nutmeg said. 'They're home already.' The Nutmouses could hear the children talking. They listened anxiously, wondering when they would discover that the helicopter and chocolates had gone.

'They might not notice,' Nutmeg said.

But they did. Arthur had left the helicopter on the kitchen table before leaving for school that morning, and he had been looking forward to getting back to it all day. So he spotted at once that it was missing.

He hunted all round the cottage, but he couldn't find it anywhere.

Then Lucy decided they should both have a chocolate, to take their minds off the missing helicopter. But

23

when she took the box down from the dresser, she found that there was not a single chocolate left.

The children stared at the empty box in astonishment. Who could have taken them? It couldn't have been their father, because Mr Mildew didn't like chocolates. He was very peculiar like that.

'We'd better ask Dad if anyone else has been in the house today,' Arthur said. 'I'll bet that whoever took these chocolates has stolen the helicopter too.'

'All right,' Lucy said. 'But let's check upstairs first, to make sure there's nothing else missing.'

So the children ran up to their bedroom in the attic, and had a good look round. But everything seemed to be in place. The toy train and the tin soldiers and the chess set were set up on the floor, just as they had left them that morning. Nothing had been touched.

'Well, it doesn't look like anyone's been up here,' Arthur said.

But then Lucy saw the doll's house,

and let out a yell: 'Arthur, quick! Look over here!'

The children kneeled down and peered inside in astonishment. The front door of the doll's house had been knocked off its hinges, and most of the furniture had gone. The sofa and chairs, the piano and the cooker, the beds, the bath—even the coat stand was missing!

'Someone must have come up here while we were at school and burgled it,' Lucy said. 'But who would want to burgle a doll's house?'

The children were very puzzled, and a little frightened too. They looked at all the rooms of the doll's house very closely, in case the thief had left any clues behind. But there was nothing to see other than the smashed in door and the broken banister rail.

'I don't like this,' Lucy said. 'We'd better go and ask Dad if anyone's been in the house while we were at school. Come on, he's in his study.'

But then Arthur spotted something. 'Wait!' he said. 'Look at this.' He was holding up a tiny white hair, which he

had plucked off the hall carpet. And once he had found one hair, he kept finding more. There were four in the bathroom, and five on the stairs, and eight in the drawing room ... in fact the whole doll's house was covered in them. And they were all as white as snow.

The children examined them in silence.

*'They're mouse hairs!'* Arthur whispered.

Lucy nodded. They had had adventures with mice before, so they knew what strange creatures they could be. And they knew that mice could be very wicked.

'A mouse would have been able to fly the toy helicopter—it's just the right size,' Arthur said excitedly. 'It must have flown up on to the dresser and stolen the chocolates, and flown up here and burgled the doll's house too! But a mouse couldn't have carried all the furniture on its own. There must be at least two of them.'

'But where could they be hiding?' Lucy wondered. 'You've already

27

searched the whole cottage up and down.'

'Perhaps they flew outside,' Arthur said anxiously. 'Dad often leaves the back door open—and they could have got out through that broken window.'

'But they can't have got far,' Lucy said. 'They would only have been able to fit a few pieces of furniture in the helicopter at a time, so they would have had to make lots of trips back and forth from the doll's house to wherever they're hiding. And besides, it's been raining all day. I reckon they must be hiding everything *inside* the cottage.'

Arthur looked thoughtful. He supposed Lucy was right; it had been a very blustery November day—not at all the sort of weather for flying a toy helicopter outdoors.

'I'll search the cottage again,' he said.

This time, Lucy helped him. They hunted upstairs and downstairs, peering under the beds, and poking behind the furniture, until at last they reached the kitchen. Arthur looked in the larder, while Lucy went through the cupboards. Finally, she tweaked aside the little gingham curtain under the sink. But all she could see were some old detergent bottles, and a pile of filthy dishcloths. She wrinkled her nose, for there was a nasty smell. *Well, there's nothing in there*, she thought, and she let the curtain drop.

'It's no good,' Arthur said, coming out of the larder. 'I can't even find a mouse dropping. Perhaps it wasn't mice after all. We'll have to tell Dad about it, and see what he thinks we should do.'

'Oh, no, don't let's tell him yet,' Lucy said. 'He'll only interfere. Let's see if we can catch the burglars ourselves. They *must* be mice—else how do you explain those white hairs we found in the doll's house? Well, we're sure to find them in the end, and it will be much be more fun to solve the mystery on our own.'

'All right,' Arthur agreed. 'Let's keep the whole thing a secret for now, and go on looking for clues.'

But Arthur was impatient to get his helicopter back. And as the evening wore on, his impatience grew. Where could the thieves be hiding? If only he could hunt them out.

Shortly before bedtime, he had an idea. *That's it!* he thought, jumping up in delight. 'Oh, *why* didn't I think of it before? I know how to catch them!'

# Chapter Four

Arthur was delighted with his plan. He would give the mice just the sort of punishment they deserved—by catching them in his toy police station! It would be just the right size, and they would never be able to nibble their way out, because the bars were made of tin.

He ran upstairs at once and dug it out of his toy box. He hadn't played with the police station for ages, and he wanted to make sure it was still working. It was a very clever toy, because it had a special booby trap—a tiny tripwire, so thin you could hardly see it. The wire was set just inside the police station, and when a toy walked into it, the wire pulled down the tin bars—*Clang!*—so the toy was locked in.

It worked very well with small dolls and toy soldiers. So it was sure to work with a mouse too.

Arthur put the police station on the floor, and gave it a test. The trap still worked perfectly, and all the tin bars

looked as good as new.

He decided not to say anything about it to Lucy. She'd only find something to fuss about. He would put the police station somewhere she wouldn't notice it, and surprise her in the morning.

Later that evening, when Lucy was getting ready for bed, he crept down to the kitchen to find a little morsel of food to lure the mice into his trap. There was no cheese, so instead he took a chunk of pastry from the chicken pie they had been eating at supper. He put the pastry just inside the police station, in front of the sergeant's desk. Then he checked the wire again, and tucked his trap under the big oak chest in the hall.

As he did so, he felt a sudden shiver of excitement. *They must be very cunning mice to steal a helicopter and raid a chocolate box and burgle a doll's house, he thought. I wonder what they'll look like.*

\* \* \*

Tumtum and Nutmeg, meanwhile, had

spent an anxious afternoon in Nutmouse Hall, listening to the children crashing around, looking for their missing toys.

Nutmeg wanted to dash out and deliver the letter to them at once, so that they would know where everything was hidden. But Tumtum wouldn't let her.

'How many times have I told you, dear. *You can't let the children see you*,' he said wearily. 'We must wait until they have gone to bed.'

Nutmeg sighed. She knew Tumtum was right, but the afternoon seemed to drag on forever. She bustled about in the kitchen, trying to take her mind off things. And after supper, she and Tumtum sat up late in the library, drinking cocoa and solving the crossword puzzle in The Mouse Times.

Finally, at ten o'clock, they heard Mr Mildew going upstairs. They waited a while, to give him time to go to bed, then they crept out under the dresser. The kitchen lights had been turned off, and it was very dark. Tumtum looked anxiously towards the sink, but there was not a sound coming from the Goldfangs. Everything was quiet. Tumtum turned on his torch, and they set off across the kitchen floor.

Nutmeg had the children's letter tucked in her apron pocket. She skipped along in front, such was her hurry to get upstairs. It was two whole days since she had last been to the attic, and she had lots to do. As well as delivering her letter, she wanted to dust out the children's satchels, and check their homework, and darn Lucy's tights, and polish Arthur's spectacles ... *And I should think the doll's house is in a terrible mess after the burglary, she thought busily. I hope I'll have time to put things straight.*

'Slow down, dear,' Tumtum panted. But Nutmeg had already scuttled on into the hall. When Tumtum caught up with her, he found her standing in the middle of the rug, twitching her nose excitedly.

'I can smell something,' she said, licking her lips. 'Mmm! It *does* smell nice!'

Then Tumtum twitched his nose, and smelled it too. Mmm! It did smell

rather delicious! *I wonder what it could be*, he thought hungrily.

He flashed his torch round the floor, trying to find where the smell was coming from. And suddenly he saw the lump of golden pastry under the chest.

'Goodness me!' he exclaimed, shining his torch at it. 'It's a big chunk of pastry! How very strange! I wonder how it got there.'

'Well, the Mildews won't be wanting it any more,' Nutmeg said. 'I'd better pick it up before the Goldfangs steal it.'

She ran across the rug. But it was only as Nutmeg was stooping to pick the pastry from the floor, that Tumtum spotted the thin walls of the police station on either side of her.

'Nutmeg! STOP!' he cried.

But it was too late. There was a tiny squeak as the bars began to scrape down—then a *CLANG!* that echoed all around the hall.

# Chapter Five

Tumtum dropped his torch to the floor and ran under the chest. Nutmeg had jumped back in fright when she stepped into the tripwire—and instead of locking her inside the police station, the tin bars had landed on top of her!

She was lying motionless, making no sound.

'Nutmeg!' Tumtum gulped, clutching her paw. It felt cold and lifeless, and for a moment he feared the very worst. But when he buried his nose in her face, he felt her eyelids flutter.

Tumtum groped for his torch, and shone it over her. He could see now that she had had a very narrow escape. Instead of hitting her on the head, the bars had fallen on her left leg, catching her just above the ankle. It was lucky she had been wearing her thick winter boots, which had given her some protection. But even so, Tumtum could see that she was in terrible pain. There was blood on her tights, and her leg was twisted.

'Oh, Tumtum, what happened?' she murmured faintly.

'You walked into a toy police station, dear,' Tumtum said, kissing her nose fondly. 'And you very nearly got trapped! But I'm going to carry you home and you shall be just fine.'

He seized the bottom of the tin bars with his paws, and tried to lift them. But they were very heavy, and though he heaved until the sweat poured down his forehead, the bars did not budge.

Tumtum stood back a moment, gasping for air; then he braced himself and tried again.

*Grrrrrr!*

*Ahhhhhh!*

Finally, the tin bars winced up a crack, just enough for him to ease Nutmeg's leg free. Then he stooped down and pulled her on to his shoulders. Nutmeg gave a little whimper, for every movement was agony.

'It's all right, dear,' Tumtum panted; but then he froze. He could hear something upstairs. A door creaked open and light flooded down the stairs. Then Mr Mildew appeared on the landing.

Nutmeg was in so much pain she did not notice him, but Tumtum felt a stab of panic. They must get away before he saw them!

'You can't carry me all the way,' Nutmeg moaned. 'You'll have to go back to Nutmouse Hall and fetch the sleigh.'

'We don't need the sleigh,' Tumtum grunted, staggering across the hall. He could hear Mr Mildew coming down the stairs behind them:

*Thud!*

*Thud!*

*Thud!*

Tumtum dared not look round. He stumbled across the kitchen, ducking under the dresser just as Mr Mildew came through the door.

Tumtum pushed open his front gates, his heart thumping. He could hear Mr Mildew crashing about behind him, and the clatter of the kettle being placed on the stove. But Tumtum cared only about Nutmeg now.

40

He carried her back into Nutmouse Hall, and laid her on the drawing room sofa. She did not look at all well. Her nose had turned white, and her paws were clammy. But when he inspected her leg, it was not as bad as he had feared. It was badly cut and bruised, but the bone had not been broken.

Tumtum fetched some pillows and blankets from the bedroom, and made Nutmeg as comfortable as he could. Then he brought her some tea, and dressed her leg with a bandage.

'How long do you think it will be until I can move about again?' Nutmeg asked weakly.

'I can't say for sure,' Tumtum replied. 'But you've had a nasty injury. I should think you'll need to stay lying down for at least a week to allow your leg to heal properly.'

'A week!' Nutmeg groaned. A week seemed a very long time. 'I can't stay in bed a whole week, I've so much to do!' she fussed. 'I've all those blackberries to turn into jam, and I've the onions to pickle and the cockroaches to smoke . . . and I was going to start stirring the

41

Christmas pudding this week ... and who knows what sort of trouble the Goldfangs will be causing while I'm lying here!'

But there was something else troubling Nutmeg, something much more serious: 'I suppose it must have been Arthur and Lucy who put down that trap,' she said miserably. 'They must have wanted to catch us. But why?'

Nutmeg felt wretched about it. But to her astonishment, Tumtum just laughed: 'Oh, my dear Nutmeg, you don't *really* think they wanted to hurt *us*? No, no, no. That would have been the last thing on their minds. They must have seen the Goldfangs, and have been trying to catch them. Or if they haven't seen them, they must at very least have guessed that it's mice that have been causing all this mischief. But you can be sure they wouldn't have put a trap down if they'd known that you were a mouse too!'

Nutmeg looked very relieved. For of course Tumtum was quite right: Arthur and Lucy had no idea that she was a mouse. She had never admitted to it in her letters, in case it frightened them—for some humans have funny feelings about mice.

'And the children might have left other traps too,' Tumtum said ominously. 'We can't risk going out again after dark, in case we stumble into another one.'

'But what about the letter?' Nutmeg asked helplessly. 'When can we deliver it to them?'

'I'll sneak upstairs in the morning,' Tumtum said. 'It can wait until then. Anyway, I don't suppose we'll have much more trouble from the Goldfangs now. When they get wind that there are traps lying around, they'll be gone from Rose Cottage in a trice—you can be quite sure of it.'

'Oh, I do hope you're right,' Nutmeg sighed. But she still felt very anxious. Her leg ached, and her head was full of worries. Tumtum insisted she try and sleep, but her dreams were not at all peaceful that night. She tossed and turned on the sofa; and it was a strange thing, but every time she went to sleep,

44

she woke with a start, fancying she could hear the B u *z z z z z z z* of a toy helicopter.

*        *        *

The next day was a Saturday. Arthur woke first, and when he sat up in bed he saw the winter sun streaming in the window, cold and bright.

He remembered his toy police station, and felt a shiver of excitement. He wondered if he had caught anything. He slipped silently out of bed and pulled on his dressing gown. But when he crept downstairs and saw the police station, he was baffled. The bars had closed, but there was nothing inside.

And yet when he picked it up, he noticed three tiny specks of blood by the sergeant's desk. Then he saw something that made his heart stop. Lying on the floor under the oak chest there was a tiny handkerchief. Arthur picked it up, and put it on his palm. He recognised it at once. It was white, with a gold border, just like

45

the handkerchief that Nutmeg had once left behind in the doll's house. And when he held it up close, and squinted at it through his glasses, he could just make out the tiny letter 'N' embroidered in gold cotton in the corner.

*I must have caught Nutmeg!* he thought in horror.

When Arthur realised what he had done, everything started to spin. He steadied himself against the chest a moment, then he climbed upstairs to tell Lucy.

Lucy was awake now, and was looking very disappointed. 'Nutmeg didn't come last night,' she said. 'I was hoping she might have left us a letter, telling us something about—'

But then Lucy noticed that Arthur's face was white as a sheet. 'What's happened?' she said.

Arthur's voice was trembling: 'I ... I wanted to catch those mice ... but ... but ... I think I must have caught Nutmeg instead! She ... she must have got away ... but there's some blood ... and ... look—she left her hankerchief!'

Arthur passed Lucy the trap and the handkerchief so she could see for herself. 'I left it in the hall last night,' he said miserably. 'And when I went down just now, that's what I found.'

Lucy did not understand it. 'But what do you mean? What happened?' she asked.

'It was a trap,' Arthur sobbed. 'There's a tripwire inside, and the bars come down when something walks into it. You remember, we used to trap your dolls in it. Well, I put it down hoping to get those mice. But I must have caught Nutmeg instead.'

Lucy was amazed. She had had no idea what Arthur was up to. She looked at the trap in silence, still puzzled as to what could have happened.

'Well, at least she must have got away,' she said eventually. 'But the bars must have caught her as they came down—that would explain these little drops of blood. I hope she wasn't badly hurt. We shall have to write her a letter, saying we're sorry, and promising that we won't put any more traps down.'

Arthur agreed. But when he opened his satchel to find a pen, he got another fright. He had left his satchel on the floor last night, with his homework book in it. But this morning the satchel was full of tiny bits of paper. His homework book had been shredded into thousands of little pieces!

'Lucy, look!' he gasped, holding the satchel open for her to see.

The children stared in amazement. Sometimes when they opened their satchels in the morning they would find that Nutmeg had been inside them in the night—she might have corrected their homework, or tidied their pencil cases, or even left them a little present.

But she would never have done something like this!

'It must have been those horrid mice again,' Arthur said furiously. 'They must have been up here in the night when we were sleeping!'

Lucy shivered. It wasn't at all nice to think of those strange, sinister mice creeping about the bedroom floor. She wondered what spiteful thing they would do next.

'If only I hadn't hurt Nutmeg, then she'd be able to help us,' Arthur said miserably. 'But now she'll never come back.'

# Chapter Six

Tumtum and Nutmeg's day had got off to a better start.

Nutmeg's leg was much less painful, and the swelling had started to go down. She found that by leaning on Tumtum's walking stick, she could stand up and shuffle about a little on her own.

'So much for staying in bed a whole week. I shall be turning cartwheels by Tuesday,' she said stubbornly.

'You must be careful,' Tumtum fussed, steering her back to the sofa. 'You still need lots of rest, or your leg might never heal properly.'

Tumtum thought Nutmeg should stay lying down. But he had to admit that her recovery was very impressive. They both felt their spirits lifting, and Tumtum decided to make a special breakfast of porridge and scrambled eggs to celebrate.

He was busy in the kitchen for some time, for it was Nutmeg who usually did the cooking, and Tumtum didn't know where all the pots and pans were kept. Finally, everything was ready. But as he was about to take the tray through to the drawing room, he noticed that the sugar pot was empty.

Tumtum sighed. He and Nutmeg both liked a grain of sugar in their tea. He looked at his watch, wondering if it would be safe to creep out into the Mildews' kitchen and borrow some. It was only eight o'clock, and the children usually got up late on Saturday—so he decided to risk it. He swung the shopping basket over his arm, and hurried out of the broom cupboard.

But he was too late! Just as he was poking his nose out from under the dresser, Arthur and Lucy walked in. And Mr Mildew followed a moment later.

'Blow,' Tumtum muttered, ducking back into the cobwebs. Had there been only one person there, he might have risked a quick dash to the larder. But with three people, he would be sure to be seen.

*We shall have to have lemon in our*

*tea instead,* he thought sadly.

And he was about to turn back to Nutmouse Hall, when he noticed something odd about Mr Mildew's appearance. Tumtum studied him curiously. Mr Mildew always looked a little scruffy, but today he looked much worse than usual. He was still in his dressing gown, and his face was ashen.

He sat down at the table, and held his head in his hands.

Tumtum wondered what was up. Surely it wasn't to do with the stolen toys? That wouldn't make Mr Mildew look as glum as this.

The children noticed it too. 'What's wrong?' Lucy asked.

'I need to talk to you both,' Mr Mildew said. His voice sounded very grave, so the children wondered what it could be. Tumtum was curious too. He stayed crouched under the dresser, with his ears pricked.

Everyone expected something awful. But nothing could have prepared them for what came next.

Mr Mildew looked very awkward. 'I'm afraid I have some ... er ... well, some rather bad news,' he began. 'You see the thing is, we're going to have to make ... er ... well, changes. Yes, changes! That's the word.'

'What sort of changes?' Lucy asked.

Mr Mildew could not look at his children. He was staring at the table, and fiddling with a teaspoon. 'We're going to have to leave Rose Cottage,' he said finally.

There was a stunned silence. Tumtum felt his paws go cold and clammy. Arthur felt the room go blurry, as though his glasses had suddenly misted over. And Lucy's stomach rose right up into her mouth.

Tumtum and the children had lived in Rose Cottage all their lives. It was the only home they had ever known. They could not imagine leaving it, so they all stared at Mr Mildew in disbelief.

'But ... but *why*?' Lucy stammered.

'Because we can't afford to stay here,' Mr Mildew replied. 'I haven't invented anything for months, and I can't pay the bills. I've nothing left.

The only solution is to sell the cottage. I've spoken to an estate agent, and he reckons I'd get a good price for it.'

'But ... but where would we go?' Arthur asked.

'Once the cottage is sold, we'll buy somewhere smaller,' Mr Mildew replied. 'I think a flat in the town might be the answer. The agent's already sent me the details of one that looks all right. It's on the third floor, so it hasn't got a garden. But there's a balcony to sit on, and it's near the park. And I might get a job—in an office perhaps. There must be something that pays better than inventing.'

The children looked horrified. They could not imagine their father in an office. In ten years, Lucy had never seen him change his jacket. And as for the town—they sometimes went there by bus at weekends, to visit the library, or the second hand shops. And while they liked it well enough for a morning, living there would be another matter.

Arthur tried to imagine what it would be like to look out of his bedroom window in the morning, and instead of seeing the orchard and the meadow, seeing shops and traffic. He knew he wouldn't like it one bit. And Lucy thought of Nutmeg. If they left Rose Cottage, they might never hear from her again.

The thought made her voice tremble: 'We CAN'T go and live in the town,' she said. 'We've always lived here. We can't leave now!'

'I'm afraid we've no choice,' her father replied. 'You'll just have to be grown-up about it. And it might not be so bad as you think. You'll have the library and the museum—there'll be lots to do.'

The children scowled. They didn't care about the library and the museum. 'I want to stay here!' Arthur said stubbornly. But it was no use arguing. Mr Mildew's mind was made up.

'It's too unfair,' Arthur said when their father had gone back upstairs. 'We can't move to the town, it will be horrid. We'll have to go to a new school, and leave all our friends. And what will we do all day without

57

a garden?'

'And what about Nutmeg?' Lucy asked miserably. 'I bet she won't want to come and live in a flat with us. There'd be nowhere for her to hide. Oh, Arthur, we can't let it happen! We can't!'

*         *         *

Tumtum felt just as strongly. And in many ways, he had even more reason to be concerned. For if Rose Cottage was sold, the new owners would be sure to strip out the old kitchen, and put in new shelves and cupboards. And when they moved the dresser, they would find the hidden door to the broom cupboard. And when they opened it, they would discover Nutmouse Hall!

Tumtum had a sudden image of a huge human fist groping about his library, knocking his books from the shelves, and he felt his stomach lurch.

He dreaded telling Nutmeg what he had heard, but he knew he must. So he hurried straight back to Nutmouse Hall. Nutmeg was propped up on her pillows on the sofa, doing her tapestry. But when she heard Tumtum's news, she dropped her needle in fright.

'But he *can't* sell Rose Cottage!' she cried. 'Oh, Tumtum, we must stop him!'

'Oh, if only we could,' Tumtum said miserably. 'But Mr Mildew hasn't earned any money for months. Rose Cottage is all he's got to sell. And I don't know what we'll do when the new owners move in. They're sure to move the dresser, then they'll discover Nutmouse Hall!'

'Oh, Tumtum, how could you be so heartless?' Nutmeg cried. 'It doesn't matter about Nutmouse Hall. We can build another house. It's Arthur and Lucy I care about. We *can't* let them move to the town. Who would look after them there?'

Tumtum looked wretched. In truth, he dreaded the children leaving just as much as Nutmeg did. He could not imagine Rose Cottage without them. It was too lonely a thought.

But then Nutmeg said something very worrying indeed: 'I tell you now,' she announced. 'If Arthur and Lucy go and live in that beastly town, then WE ARE GOING TOO!'

# Chapter Seven

It was a miserable day in Rose Cottage. It rained all morning, and Mr Mildew locked himself up in his study, and refused to talk to his children at all. Arthur and Lucy felt sure there must be a way of keeping the cottage. But their father seemed to have given up already.

Then, just before lunch, a shiny red sports car drew up outside, and two men in grey suits climbed out. Mr Mildew came down to let them in, and he showed them all round the cottage. They were holding clipboards, and they made little notes as they went from room to room, picking their way round the piles of clutter.

Then they went into the garden with their umbrellas, and took photographs of the house from the outside.

The children peered down at them from the attic window.

'Who are they?' Lucy asked suspiciously.

'They're estate agents,' Arthur replied. 'They sell houses. They're going to put a photograph of Rose Cottage in the window of their shop, and sell it to someone awful.'

'Well, they won't get a very nice photograph in the rain,' Lucy said crossly. 'I hope it looks horrid, then no one will want to buy it, and we shan't be able to move after all.'

But the two men seemed very happy with what they had seen. When they had photographed the cottage from every angle, they clattered back inside, full of encouraging comments.

'A most charming cottage, Mr Mildew,' one of them enthused. 'Full of, er . . . period features.'

'We'll market it as "A character cottage in need of complete renovation" the other went on. 'There should be a lot of interest in a tumbledown place like this. Might appeal to someone from London, looking for somewhere to do up for the weekends.'

The children looked at each other in disgust.

'Oh, isn't it horrid!' Lucy fumed. 'Poor Rose Cottage! Fancy being *done up for the weekends*, whatever that means.'

'I suppose they'll strip out all the wonky old doors and windows, and put in new ones, and make it look just like every other boring old house,' Arthur said sourly.

'But what will Nutmeg do?' Lucy said. 'She'll hate it. Perhaps I should leave the doll's house behind for her, so she'll still have somewhere to sleep. But I don't suppose it would be any use. The new owners would probably just throw it away.'

All in all, Arthur and Lucy were feeling very miserable.

And, back in the broom cupboard, Tumtum and Nutmeg were feeling miserable too. Somehow, they had a funny feeling that Goldfang and his son Snout were contributing to their bad luck.

'Since those mice appeared in the larder, everything's gone wrong,' Nutmeg said. 'First they did those horrid things to the children, then I got

63

caught in a toy police station, which was meant for *them*. And now Mr Mildew's announced that he's going to sell Rose Cottage. Do you know, Tumtum, I think they've put a curse on us!'

'Hmmm,' Tumtum said. He did not believe in curses. But it was true that the Goldfangs had been nothing but trouble. And the sooner they were made to leave Rose Cottage, the better it would be.

'I'm going to try and deliver that letter to the children right now, telling them where the Goldfangs are hiding,' he said. 'I'm sure I can creep up to the attic without being seen.'

'But everyone's indoors—I can hear them,' Nutmeg said anxiously.

'I shall be very careful,' Tumtum said. 'I promise I shan't let anyone see me.'

Nutmeg sighed. She did not like Tumtum going out alone, but she was eager for the children to get the letter too.

'All right,' she said. 'But keep to the skirting. And when you've delivered the letter, come straight back.'

'Of course I will,' Tumtum replied.

But getting to the attic was not going to be as easy as Tumtum had hoped. For what with Mr Mildew and the estate agents and the children, there were people coming and going from the kitchen all morning long. He waited under the dresser for more than an hour, listening to everyone clattering about.

Eventually, the estate agents left. And soon afterwards, the rain stopped and the children went outside to play. Mr Mildew had gone back to his study, so Tumtum thought this would be his chance to slip upstairs unseen.

But just as he was stepping out from under the dresser, he saw something that made him jump back in fright. It was Goldfang, over on the other side of the kitchen, beside the garden door. He was pacing about on the doormat, as if waiting for something to happen.

'Blow,' Tumtum muttered, for he didn't want Goldfang following him up to attic, and reading his letter.

Tumtum wondered what he was

65

doing there. Then he heard a squeak—and next thing an enormous ginger mouse slithered in under the garden door.

Tumtum stared in astonishment, for he was the biggest mouse he had ever seen. He was as thick as a broom handle, and he had muscles like gobstoppers, bulging under a black tracksuit.

Goldfang and the ginger mouse grunted a greeting. Neither looked very pleased to see each other.

'What's this all about?' the ginger mouse asked crossly. 'I was just gettin' to sleep, then I gits a call telling me to get 'ere faster than a bleedin' grasshopper. Well, this place looks like a dump to me. So there'd better be a good reason for it all, or—'

'A very good reason, Punch,' Goldfang purred, raising his paw. '*A very good reason indeed*. But our business is Top Secret. We must talk somewhere quieter. 'Come with me and I shall explain *everything*.'

'Where are we goin'?' Punch asked suspiciously.

'To my new home, a most charming little bleach bottle,' Goldfang smiled. Then he led his guest across the kitchen, and through the little gingham curtain under the sink. They made an odd pair. Goldfang was so thin, he moved like a spider, while Punch stamped sullenly behind.

Tumtum watched them disappear, suddenly feeling very excited. He had suspected from the start that Goldfang and Snout were up to something, and this could be his chance to find out what it was.

Goldfang had said he would explain *everything*. So Tumtum decided to follow the two mice back to the bleach bottle and crouch beneath the window, trying to hear what was said.

He tiptoed to the sink, and poked his nose under the curtain. The helicopter was no longer there. He supposed Goldfang must have moved it to another hiding place. But the bleach bottle was all lit up at the back of the cupboard, and when Tumtum peered through the window, he could see the Goldfangs and Punch sitting around the doll's house table, with their heads bent.

Tumtum was too far off to hear what they were saying. So he crept right up to the house, and crouched under the window.

He pressed his handkerchief tight to his nose, for the smell of bleach made his nostrils tickle, and he was frightened he might sneeze. He heard plates being clattered on the table, then the sound of chomping jaws as the mice tucked into a late lunch.

'Cold cockroach! Eugh!' Punch snorted. 'You better 'ave a good reason for callin' me out to this stinking bleach bottle and givin' me cold cockroach for lunch.'

'I told you, *I have a very good reason indeed*,' Goldfang hissed. 'You do exactly as I say, and by tomorrow night the three of us will be the richest mice in town.'

Punch belched.

'Now listen carefully,' Goldfang growled. His voice was very low, and Tumtum had to strain his ears to follow what was said.

'We had an uncle, Old Uncle Bernie, who visited this cottage last summer,' Goldfang began. 'He ended up here by accident. He was on his way to burgle a house on the other side of the village, but Old Uncle Bernie wasn't good with a map, and he went left instead of right, and north instead of south, and he ended up here instead.

'He soon realised his mistake. But having got here, he had a quick sniff around, to see if there was anything worth nicking. Of course there wasn't much—the humans here are poor as church mice, not a silver teaspoon to their name. But before he moved on, he decided to have a look under the floorboards. He was a very thorough crook, was Old Uncle Bernie—he never left a house without checking under the floor. You never know what might have dropped—'

'All right, all right,' Punch said gruffly. He had a short attention span, and he was getting bored. 'Get to the point, Goldfang. What did he find?'

'Something *very unexpected*,' Goldfang replied mysteriously.

'WHAT?' Punch barked.

Tumtum was getting impatient too. What was it that Goldfang's uncle had found? He crouched very still, listening expectantly—and when he heard the answer, his ears went as stiff as wood.

'GOLD!' Goldfang hissed. 'He found a bag of gold coins—huge, ancient, centuries-old gold coins ... a dozen of them, and each one as heavy as a toad. A whole pile of gold—gold, *gold*, *GOLD*! Rare, priceless, beautiful, glorious GOLD! And hidden RIGHT HERE! *Under the floorboards of Rose Cottage!*'

# Chapter Eight

Tumtum could scarcely believe it. *Rare gold coins*, hidden in *Rose Cottage*! But this could solve all Mr Mildew's problems! It might mean he wouldn't have to sell Rose Cottage after all.

But the mice had other plans.

'Gold? Are you sure 'e wasn't 'avin you on?' Punch asked gruffly.

'Of course he wasn't having us on— *we've seen them!*' Snout squeaked. 'They're in a bag. They must have been hidden under the floor by some fool of a human. But it was our Old Uncle Bernie who found them—and now they're ours for the taking!'

'Why didn't your uncle take 'em with 'im?' Punch asked suspiciously.

'Because he couldn't carry them on his own,' Goldfang replied. 'And he's old now; he hasn't the strength to come back. That's why he sent us. But we need a strong mouse like you to help us lift them.'

'And what do I get?' Punch asked

greedily.

'Two gold coins,' Goldfang replied coolly. 'Two for you, and the rest for us. And you can't argue with that!'

Had Punch's maths been a little better, he might well have argued— for two gold coins out of twelve was not a big share. But even so, it would be enough to make him very rich. He was silent for a second or two, as he imagined the sort of life he might lead ... a life of hot baths, and feather beds, and glorious feasts that went on and on. Just thinking about it made him shiver.

'How do we get the gold back to town?' he asked anxiously.

'We'll fly,' Goldfang replied. 'We've got a helicopter—we stole it off the brat upstairs.'

'And when do we go?' Punch asked.

'Tomorrow, just before midnight,' Goldfang replied. 'You know the business. A sensible crook always carries out his burglaries on a Sunday night, when there aren't so many policemice on duty.'

Tumtum was listening to all this with

intense excitement. Somehow, he must make sure that Arthur and Lucy got hold of the coins before Goldfang did.

Then Punch asked the question he had been longing to hear:

'Which floorboards are the coins hidden under?'

Tumtum held his breath. But then something quite dreadful happened. At that very moment, with the cruellest timing, the Mildews' boiler started to splutter. The boiler was located just above the sink, and it was one of the old, wonky sort of boilers that splutter very loudly: *Aaaaagh! Grrrrrr! Clonk! Clank! Rrrrrrrrr!*

And to Tumtum's dismay, he did not hear Goldfang's reply. He waited tensely, until finally the boiler stopped. But by then the conversation inside the beach bottle had moved on. The mice had started talking about the route they would take when they flew the helicopter back to town.

'Blast,' Tumtum muttered, clenching his fist.

Then suddenly he heard a chair scrape as one of the mice got up from the table. 'I'm going out for a cigar,' Goldfang said—and next moment a thin black shadow spilled from the bleach bottle's front door.

Tumtum was terrified he would be seen. If the mice found him here, and realised he had discovered their secret, they would never let him go.

Hardly daring to breathe, he slunk back against the cupboard wall, and crept to the curtain. Then he wriggled under it, and ran straight back to Nutmouse Hall.

He was trembling all over, both from excitement and fear. Arthur and Lucy's letter could wait. First he wanted to tell Nutmeg everything that he had heard.

She listened to his story in astonishment.

'Gold hidden in Rose Cottage! Oh, Tumtum, who would have thought it!' she gasped. 'I knew those mice must have had a secret reason for being here, and now we know what it is! We must write a new letter to the children at once, telling them where the gold is hidden!'

'But that's just the problem,'

Tumtum groaned. 'I didn't find out where the coins are. All I know is that they're under a floorboard somewhere in Rose Cottage. But when Goldfang said which floorboard it was, the boiler started to rumble—*and I didn't hear!*'

'Blow,' Nutmeg said. 'The whole cottage is covered in floorboards. The coins could be under any one of them. And the boards are nailed down. It would take the children weeks to pull them all up. Unless we can tell them exactly where the coins are hidden, I doubt they would ever be able to find them by tomorrow night.'

'Well, we can at least tell them where the mice are hiding, so they can try and catch them,' Tumtum said. 'But I suppose it might not be as easy as all that. There are three mice now— it will be hard to catch them all. And I noticed that they've made a little watchtower at the top of the bleach bottle. They obviously plan to keep their guard.'

Nutmeg nodded. 'Thieves like that would be too clever to get caught,' she said. 'And if they've moved the helicopter to another hiding place, then they're obviously not taking any chances. Anyway, we don't want to alarm them. They said they're planning to steal the gold tomorrow night, but if we frighten them, they might carry out the burglary even sooner.'

Tumtum agreed. It wouldn't do to alarm Goldfang now. They needed to outwit him.

But how?

They both thought very hard. Then Nutmeg suddenly clapped her paws in delight: 'Oh, Tumtum, why didn't we think of it before?' she cried. 'General Marchmouse can help us! Don't you remember, dear? Mrs Marchmouse gave him a metal detector for his last birthday! He showed me how it works when we last went over there for dinner. It's most awfully clever. You run it along the ground like a vacuum cleaner, and when it detects metal, it goes, "Beep!" It will lead us to the gold in no time! We can ask the General to bring it to Rose Cottage tonight, then you and he can go round all the rooms while the Goldfangs and Punch are asleep. And once you've found the gold, we can tell the children *exactly* where it's hidden.'

Tumtum agreed that it was a splendid plan. 'And we needn't worry about stumbling into that toy police station again,' he said. 'Because the metal detector will detect that too!'

They both laughed. Suddenly things didn't look nearly so bleak.

'Won't the children be thrilled when they learn there's gold hidden in Rose Cottage!' Nutmeg said excitedly. 'Oh, do hurry, dear! Let's fetch General Marchmouse at once!'

Tumtum set off without delay. The children were still outside, so he was able to dart across the kitchen unseen. Then he wriggled under the garden door, and hurried down the path to the lane.

The clouds had blown away, and it had turned into a crisp autumn afternoon. Tumtum doffed his cap to a butterfly and started humming a cheerful tune. Things were looking up at last. They had discovered Goldfang's secret, and they were sure to find the gold tonight with the help of General Marchmouse and his metal detector.

He cut across the lawn, beating through the long grass and the dead leaves, and scrambled under the hedge into the Manor House garden.

It was a very big garden, but Tumtum knew just where he wanted to go. He trekked through the orchard and the vegetable patch, then clambered up

81

the creeper on the side of the house, and wriggled through the broken windowpane in to the downstairs cloakroom.

Once inside, he dropped on to the lavatory seat, and slid down the loo brush to the floor. Finally, he raced down the long tiled corridor to the gunroom.

There were no guns in the gunroom any more, because the owner of the Manor House, Mr Stirrup, had given up shooting long ago, when his eyesight started to fail. He had not set foot in the gunroom for years, so the General and Mrs Marchmouse lived there undisturbed. Their home was a handsome gun cupboard, nearly two metres tall.

Tumtum could see they were in, for there was light glinting from the keyhole. He hurried up to the front door, and gave a loud *Rat-tat.*

The General was delighted to see his friend. He had spent the afternoon polishing his medals, and he was ready for a bit of fun.

'Nutmouse, old boy! Come in, come

in!' he cried, ushering him inside. 'You're just in time for tea!'

And before he could say a word, Tumtum was whisked through to the kitchen, where he found Mrs Marchmouse taking a tray of hot scones from the oven.

'Scones! Hooray!' the General said gleefully. 'We shall have them with jam and cream! And there are crab sandwiches and ginger biscuits too! It's hungry work polishing medals when you've as many as me!'

The General was in a very boisterous mood, and it was some minutes before Tumtum had a chance to tell him why he had come. When the General finally listened to Tumtum's story, his face glowed with excitement. A secret stash of gold! A stolen helicopter! Villains with gold fangs! This sounded just the sort of adventure he liked.

'Goldfang plans to make off with the gold coins tomorrow night,' Tumtum explained. 'But we were hoping that if you came to Rose Cottage with your metal detector, we might be able to find them first!'

Tumtum was worried the General might consider the plan too dangerous. But he should have known better. For the General adored danger, and he was grinning from ear to ear.

'Oh, yes, I shall come all right!' he cried. 'And I shall arrest those thieving mice while I'm at it! I'll hunt them down in a toy tank, and march them through the village in handcuffs! Oh, how the field-mice will cheer!'

The General stuffed another scone into his mouth, feeling very pleased with himself.

But Tumtum looked stern. 'I warn you, General, Goldfang is a very *dangerous* mouse. He's already bombed me with a peanut, and he might do worse. Your job is simply to find where the gold is hidden. You aren't to try any clever tricks. And if Goldfang sees you, you're to run as fast as you can.'

The General snorted. He had never run from an enemy in his life. But there was no time for an argument now. It was nearly four o'clock, and Tumtum wanted to be home before it grew dark. So they hurriedly finished their tea,

then the General fetched his metal detector from the study, and he and Tumtum set off back to Rose Cottage.

Mrs Marchmouse waved them off from the door, looking rather forlorn. Poor Mrs Marchmouse didn't much care for adventures. But she knew there was no point trying to stop her husband from going. *Generals will be Generals*, she thought wistfully, as she watched him disappear behind a gun boot.

It was a long way back across the garden, and the light was fading fast. Tumtum and the General hurried as fast as they could, but by the time they crept under the garden door into Rose Cottage the sky had turned black.

Tumtum hovered on the mat, peering nervously around the kitchen. The light was on, but everything was quiet. The only sound was the faint *Clank! Clonk!* of Mr Mildew's typewriter, carrying down from the study. Arthur and Lucy's coats were back on their pegs, so Tumtum supposed they must be upstairs.

'Come on, let's get back to

Nutmouse Hall,' he said.

But the General wanted to start work. 'I'd better get going,' he said impatiently. 'There are a lot of floorboards in this cottage. I'm going to need all the time we've got.'

'But you can't start now,' Tumtum said anxiously. 'If the children come downstairs they might see you. You must wait until everyone's gone to bed.'

'But I must start now, or I might not find the coins before morning,' the General replied stubbornly. 'I'll do the drawing room first. I'll creep about under the chairs and cupboards. The children won't see me.'

Tumtum frowned. He thought it was very risky for the General to set out with his metal detector when everyone was still awake. But it was true that there were a lot of floorboards to cover.

'All right then,' he said eventually. 'I'll go and tell Nutmeg that we've got back safely, then I'll come and see how you're getting on.'

So the General marched off to the drawing room, while Tumtum hurried back to Nutmouse Hall. He had been gone several hours, and Nutmeg was relieved to see him. But when he told her that the General had already begun his search, she looked anxious.

'He promised he'd be careful,' Tumtum reassured her. 'I'll go back in a moment and see how he's getting on. But first I'm going to bring you something to eat. You need to keep your strength up.'

Nutmeg smiled. She knew she was lucky having Tumtum to look after her. He disappeared to the kitchen, and a few moments later he reappeared with some fish paste sandwiches and a large slice of apple pie. Tumtum had some too, for he was very hungry after his long walk. Then he set off to see how the General was getting on.

But when he peeked out from under the dresser, he saw something that made him jump back in fright.

It was those wretched mice again! And they were in a toy jeep—stolen from Arthur's toy barracks!

The jeep had pulled up under the kitchen table. It was pointing towards the hall, with its roof wound back.

Goldfang was standing up in the front seat, peering over the windscreen through a pair of binoculars. Snout was sitting next to him, and Punch was squeezed in the back.

The two older mice were dressed in black, but Snout was wearing an officer's uniform stolen from a toy soldier.

Tumtum kept very still, watching to see what happened next.

'He went that way!' Snout squealed, jabbing his paw ahead. 'And he was dressed in a uniform, Dad! Honest, he was!'

'What sort of uniform?' Goldfang hissed.

'It had red and green stripes,' Snout said excitedly. 'It looked like the Royal Mouse Army Uniform!'

'*THE ROYAL MOUSE ARMY!*' Goldfang gave a furious snarl, as if the thought of the Royal Mouse Army was a truly terrible thing. 'And what was he doing?'

'It looked like 'e was pushing a vacuum cleaner,' said Punch, who had seen him too.

'An army mouse, *pushing a vacuum cleaner?*' Goldfang snorted. 'Pah! I don't believe it! He's up to something. Come on, let's grab him!'

Goldfang sat down in the seat, and pressed a red knob on the dashboard. The jeep sprang to life, and sped towards the hall.

Tumtum watched in dismay. They were going to seize the General! *I must get a warning to him*, he thought desperately.

He waited until the jeep had disappeared round the kitchen door, then he crept out from under the dresser, and tiptoed after it. When he peeked into the hall, he saw it jolting to a stop by the drawing room door. Then the three mice clambered out, and started advancing silently towards the sofa.

'Are you sure you saw him?' Goldfang snarled, peering under the sofa with his field glasses.

'I promise I did!' Snout squealed. 'I'm telling you, it was a mouse dressed in army uniform!'

'I saw 'im too,' Punch said grimly.

'He must be 'ere somewhere.'

They crept on, round the sofa, and under the armchair. But it was Tumtum who spotted the General first. He slipped out from the under the drawing room door, and climbed on top of a footstool, so he could see all round the room.

And there the General was— searching round the log basket with his metal detector! His tail was wagging, and his ears were twitching excitedly, waiting for the machine to beep.

Tumtum waved his arms frantically, trying to get his attention. But the General had his eyes down. He was in a world of his own. He had already covered half of the drawing room, and he felt sure he was going to find the gold coins soon. *'Hey, ho, hey, ho, it's a treasure hunting we go!'* he hummed happily, as he slid his metal detector over the floor.

He went all around the log basket, and started inching towards the bookshelf. *Oh, how thrilling it is to be on a real treasure hunt!* he thought gleefully. *Just think what a fuss* The

Mouse Times *will make when they hear that the Great General Marchmouse has discovered a stash of Long Lost Gold! They'll be sure to put my picture on the front page!*

Such were the joyful thoughts crowding his head when suddenly:

*Beep! Beep!*

*BEEP! BEEP!*

The General's heart gave a thump. He had found something at last! And it was surely something big, because the beeps were getting louder and louder:

*BEEP! BEEP!*

*BEEP! BEEP!*

*BEEP! BEEP!*

*BEEP! BEEP!*

He jumped with excitement. It must be the gold coins!

He slid the metal detector round the floor again, trying to find where the noise was loudest. But it made no

92

difference. Whichever way he turned, the machine beeped louder and louder.

Then the General heard a patter of paws on the carpet.

'Nutmouse, thank goodness you're back! Come quick, I've found something!' he shouted excitedly. 'Listen to the old metal detector. She's beeping like billy-o! It must be the gold coins. Oh, come on, hurry, old boy! They must be buried RIGHT HERE!'

The machine was shrieking now, and throbbing in his paws. But then suddenly the General heard a growl—and when he turned round he saw a sight that chilled the blood in his tail.

It was a huge lump of gold. But it wasn't a coin. It was a gold fang, as sharp as a dagger. And it was inside the mouth of the nastiest looking mouse he had ever seen.

'How do you do?' Goldfang snarled—and off the little metal detector went again: *Beep! Beep! Beep! Beep! Beep! Beep . . . Beep!*

# Chapter Ten

The General felt his legs quiver. He remembered the advice that Tumtum had given him: 'Goldfang is a very dangerous mouse. If you meet him, you must *run . . . run . . . RUN!*'

But somehow he couldn't.

Snout and Punch had also appeared, and the three mice were staring at the General very coldly.

'How do you do? I am General Marchmouse,' he said stiffly. He held out his paw, but no one took it.

The Goldfangs and Punch all had a funny feeling they had seen the General before. And well they might, for General Marchmouse was very famous. His picture often appeared in *The Mouse Times*, and his face had been on a Christmas stamp. But Goldfang and his friends didn't read the newspapers, so they didn't recognise him as quickly as other mice might have done.

It was Snout who got there first.

'Hey! I know who you are!' he squeaked. 'I've seen your face on the Royal Mouse Army recruiting posters! General Marchmouse, that's right. You're that pompous old fool from the Squirrel Regiment.'

The General spluttered. His face turned crimson, and his whiskers went as stiff as wire. He wasn't frightened now.

'You young pipsqueak!' he barked, poking him in the chest. 'How *dare* you talk to a senior officer like that! And what the devil are you doing dressed in that cavalry uniform? You're not an army mouse. Give me your name, and I shall have you arrested for impersonating an officer!'

Usually mice trembled when General Marchmouse shouted at them. But Snout just sneered.

'You are a disgrace to the breed,' the General shouted. 'A few months in the Royal Mouse Army would knock some manners into you.'

'The Royal Mouse Army. Oh, tee, hee!' Snout giggled. 'The army's for fools.'

And as he giggled, the metal detector gave another loud beep.

Goldfang was looking at it suspiciously. 'What is it?' he snarled.

At the sight of Goldfang's teeth, the General started feeling nervous again. 'It . . . it . . . it's a vacuum cleaner!' he stammered, clutching it nervously. 'I . . . I was just cleaning up some crumbs I spilled . . . Well, you see . . . er . . . one . . . one doesn't want to leave traces.'

Goldfang was not so easily fooled. 'Give it to me!' he growled, snatching it from the General's paws.

But as he took hold of it, the machine started shrieking and throbbing so violently that Goldfang dropped it in fright.

'It's witchcraft!' he cried. 'Take it away!'

''Ang on a minute,' said Punch. He picked the metal detector up from the floor, and turned it upside down, examining it all over. 'This ain't witchcraft,' he said in astonishment. 'It's a bleedin' metal detector.'

The expression on Goldfang's face was horrible to behold. His eyes narrowed into two thin black slits, and his gold fang glinted.

'A metal detector!' he hissed. 'And pray tell me, General Marchmouse, what are you looking for?' His voice was teasing, but so cold that the General felt his stomach lurch.

'I ... er ... well, I was just looking for ... er ... little bits of metal!' the General mumbled. And because he was nervous, he started to babble: 'I, well, I was just looking for this and that. Never know what you might find in an old cottage like this. A penny here, a ha'penny there. Why! Once I found a ten-pence piece, so big I had to pull it home on my sleigh, and last Christmas my old friend Mr Nutmouse found a silver charm, fallen out of the plum pudding ...'

'*Mr Nutmouse!*' Goldfang barked. 'Is that the old fool we saw in the larder?'

'Well, er, I couldn't be sure,' the General squirmed. And sensing he had already said too much, he made his excuses: 'Now if you'll excuse me, I had better scamper off home. Goodness me, look at the time! I shall be late for supper.'

The General held out his paw to Punch, hoping to get his machine back. But Punch, in grim silence, put the metal detector across his knee, and snapped it in two.

'H-how dare you?' the General gasped—but Goldfang waved him quiet.

'We know your game, General Marchmouse. You're after the gold coins. Well, we'll teach you not to meddle in our treasure hunt. Now take us to your friend Nutmouse, and we'll lock you both up together!'

Suddenly, the General was aware of Punch lunging towards him ... and of Goldfang pulling out a gun.

He heard Tumtum's words again— 'Run! Run! *RUN*!'—and this time he did, leaping like a cricket towards the drawing room door.

The General could hear the three mice pounding after him. Then a shot rang out, and a volley of hundreds and thousands peppered him in the rear.

'Ouch!' he cried, tearing into the hall.

'Give yourself up!' Goldfang roared. But the General hurtled on.

Tumtum had dived back under the door so as not to be seen. He tried to signal to the General as he passed him—*'Pssst! Under here!'*—but the General did not hear.

He raced blindly into the kitchen. Then he heard a roar, and when he looked round he let out a shriek. They were coming after him in the jeep.

*R-r-r-r-r-r-r-r-r-r-!*

'We've got you now!' Goldfang shrieked.

*Vroom! Vroom!*
*Vroom! Vroom!*

The General fled across the floor in terror. But then he heard a sudden screech of brakes, and when he looked back he saw the jeep skid on a pool of grease, and smash into a table leg.

*Crrrrunch!*

Its little tin bonnet crumpled like a sheet of paper, and smoke poured from the engine.

The General seized his chance, and dived under the dresser. And when he looked back he saw the three mice

staggering from the vehicle, looking very battered.

Punch had a broken tail, and Goldfang and Snout were both rubbing their noses.

'Where did he go?' Goldfang demanded.

'That way,' Punch grunted, pointing towards the larder.

'Then let's find him,' Goldfang hissed. And off they all stormed, in quite the wrong direction.

The General breathed a deep sigh. He knew he'd had a very lucky escape. He had not seen Tumtum in the drawing room, so he assumed that he was still in Nutmouse Hall. He decided to go back in at once, and tell him what had happened.

But just as the General was hurrying back into the broom cupboard, Tumtum crept into the kitchen. Everything was very quiet, and he wondered where everyone was.

*They must have caught the General, and taken him back to the bleach bottle*, he thought anxiously.

But then he saw the jeep lying

crumpled against the table leg. *Gracious me!* he exclaimed. Tumtum hurried over to it, wondering if anyone was lying injured inside. But the windows were too high for him to see in. So he pulled open the door, and clambered up into the front seat.

The jeep was empty. But Tumtum could see that it had been a nasty crash. The steering wheel was dented, and the gearstick had been snapped in two. He paused a moment to inspect the damage, wondering if he would be able to repair it with his tool kit.

Then he heard a click. And when he looked up he saw to his fright that the roof of the jeep had suddenly snapped shut on him.

He felt the seat lurch—and next thing he knew, the jeep was flying into the air. He saw a pink thumb press down on the windscreen. Then a huge pink nose appeared at the window, and in peered Arthur, looking very, VERY cross.

# Chapter Eleven

Arthur had not seen any of the other mice. So he assumed everything was Tumtum's fault.

'Lucy, come down here, quick!' he shouted. 'You won't believe what I've found!' Lucy came running downstairs. And when Arthur showed her the jeep, with the little mouse trapped inside, she was astonished.

'He was trying to steal it, but he crashed into the table leg,' Arthur said excitedly. 'And it must have been him who stole the chocolates and the helicopter and burgled the doll's house and ate my homework. What a wicked mouse, to be sure!'

Lucy looked at Tumtum. It certainly seemed that he had been up to a lot of mischief. But somehow he didn't look as wicked as all that. He was dressed in corduroy trousers and a tattered tweed jacket. And he had a pair of spectacles perched on the end of his nose. Lucy thought he looked rather endearing.

'Oh, but my dear children, it wasn't me!' Tumtum cried, pressing his nose to the window. 'Don't you see, there has been a terrible misunderstanding! It's the Goldfangs who stole everything! And now they're going to steal the gold too! Oh, please! You must let me go, or we'll never stop them!'

Tumtum bashed on the window, and shouted as loudly as he could, desperately trying to make the children understand. But it was no good. His voice was so tiny, all they could hear was a squeal.

They wondered what to do with him. Arthur was feeling unforgiving. 'This mouse has done enough harm already—and if we don't get rid of him, he might do something even worse,' he said. 'Let's take him down to Blackdown Wood, and tip him out there. 'Then you can be sure he'll never find his way back to Rose Cottage!'

Tumtum let out a yelp. He had never been to Blackdown Wood, but he had heard all sorts of terrifying stories about it. It was on the other side of the churchyard, and in parts of it the trees grew so thick you couldn't see the sky. It was full of owls and foxes, and there were said to be ghosts there too.

'Oh, please, please, don't take me to Blackdown Wood,' he begged, looking up pleadingly through the windscreen. 'I'll be eaten alive!'

Arthur was unmoved. But Lucy was looking at Tumtum thoughtfully. He seemed such a sad, earnest little mouse. Somehow she couldn't believe that it was him who had done all the bad things.

'We can't be *sure* it was this mouse who robbed us,' she said carefully. 'After all, we haven't got any proper evidence. And we know there must have been two mice, remember, not just one. This mouse couldn't have moved all that furniture from the doll's house on his own. And besides, the hairs we found were all white. And this mouse is brown.'

Arthur looked sulky. He hadn't thought of this. 'Well, all right then, there must be a white mouse as well,' he said grudgingly. 'But that doesn't mean this mouse isn't guilty too.'

'I think we should keep him safe, and ask Nutmeg what to do with him. She might know if he's really to blame or not,' Lucy said.

'There's no point asking Nutmeg,' Arthur replied. 'She hasn't been to see us for ages.'

'Well, that's only because you frightened her away with that silly trap,' Lucy said sharply.

It might have turned into a row. But next moment, the children heard Mr Mildew coming downstairs. They looked at each other anxiously. They didn't want to show their father what they had found. He would be amazed if he saw a mouse in a tweed jacket, and he would start interfering—but they wanted to solve the mystery on their own.

'Let's take him outside,' Arthur said. So they hurried into the garden, carrying Tumtum in the jeep.

'I've an idea,' Lucy said. 'Let's put him in that old fish tank in the garden shed. Dad will never find him there,

107

and he won't be able to cause any more trouble. He's such an odd-looking mouse, we can't just let him go.'

Arthur agreed to this, so they took the torch from the shelf and carried Tumtum outside.

It was a moonless night, and the shed was pitch black inside. But Tumtum could see the fish tank in the torch beam, and he didn't like the look of it one bit. It was on a shelf high up at the back of the shed, and to Tumtum its walls seemed as tall as towers. Lucy had kept a goldfish in the tank long ago, but it would be no good for a fish now. The glass was splintered, and the walls were black with dust.

Arthur waited while Lucy ran back to the house to fetch a saucer of crumbs, and an egg-cup full of water. She also found an old football sock for the mouse to lie on. Arthur shone the torch into the tank while she placed everything inside. Then they gently lowered in the jeep, and tipped Tumtum from it.

He came tumbling out upside down, and in his confusion he stumbled into the egg cup, and got his trousers soaked.

'Oh, please don't leave me here!' he cried, peering up at them in the torchlight. 'Nutmeg won't know where I am—she'll be worried sick. And those three wicked mice will escape with the gold coins tomorrow night! Oh, children, don't you know . . . *THERE'S GOLD BURIED UNDER YOUR FLOORBOARDS!*'

But the children didn't know, of course. And however loud Tumtum shouted, he couldn't make them hear.

The little mouse looked so distressed, even Arthur felt sorry for him. 'Don't you worry. We'll come and feed you again in the morning,' he promised. Then the children left him all alone.

\*          \*          \*

Meanwhile, back inside Rose Cottage, Nutmeg and General Marchmouse had been involved in a very unpleasant adventure of their own.

After his escape from Goldfang,

110

the General had rushed straight back to Nutmouse Hall, expecting to find Tumtum there. But he wasn't.

'He's not here,' Nutmeg said, looking up anxiously from her sewing. 'He left nearly an hour ago, to look for you.'

The General frowned. He hadn't seen Tumtum in Rose Cottage, so where could he be? He hoped he hadn't got into difficulties of some kind. And seeing how worried Nutmeg was, he set off at once to look for him.

The General felt sure Goldfang and the others wouldn't give him any more trouble now. They would be licking their wounds after their crash.

But as he was about to open the front gates, and slip back out of the broom cupboard, he heard a sudden clatter—and when he looked up, he saw a toy bulldozer thundering under the dresser!

*Clonk! Clank! R r r r r r r!*

The General stared at it in horror. It was heading straight for the gates!

He stood rooted to the ground with fear. He wanted to run, but his legs

felt numb. Finally, he gathered his wits and fled back into Nutmouse Hall, clanging the bolts behind him. He heard a terrible crash, and when he peeked through the letterbox, he saw the bulldozer smashing the gates from their hinges.

*Crrrrrrunch!*

Then on it came, grinding towards the front door! And he could see the Goldfangs and Punch glaring through the windscreen.

The General ran into the drawing room. Nutmeg had heard the noise, and risen from the sofa in alarm.

'Whatever's going on?' she cried, hobbling on her walking stick.

'Arm yourself with a knitting needle!' the General shouted. 'They've broken into the broom cupboard!'

And suddenly the whole room shook, as the toy bulldozer smashed through the front door.

# Chapter Twelve

Nutmeg and the General listened in terror as the bulldozer crashed into the hall. They heard doors slamming, and footsteps thundering down the passage—then the drawing room door was flung open, and the Goldfangs and Punch rushed in.

'Hah! We'll teach you what happens to mice who meddle in our Top Secret affairs!' Goldfang snarled. 'We're going to lock you up in the cellar!'

'Oh, no you're NOT!' the General roared. He grabbed a poker from the fireplace, and made to stab Goldfang in the stomach. But Punch seized him by the scruff of the neck, and dragged him to the door.

'Let him go!' Nutmeg cried. *'How dare you smash into my house!* This is private property. When Chief Constable Watchmouse hears about this, he'll send you all to the mouse prison!'

Snout gave a snort. 'And who's going

to call Chief Constable Watchmouse?' he asked mockingly. 'Not your husband, that's for sure. He's been caught stealing a toy jeep! Arthur and Lucy have *locked him up!*'

This was the first Nutmeg had heard of Tumtum's misadventure, and she was distraught. *'The children have caught Tumtum?'* she gasped. 'Are you sure? Where did they take him? Did you see?'

But no one would tell her anything more.

'Lock them up,' Goldfang barked.

Punch dragged the General down the corridor, while the Goldfangs followed behind, pushing Nutmeg along on her crutches. Then they shoved them both inside the cellar, and bolted the door.

'Let us out!' the General shouted. 'Let us out or I'll set the Royal Mouse Army after you.'

But there was no reply. They could just hear the thieves' footsteps fading down the passage. The cellar was very dark, and they were all alone.

'Oh, General, what are we to do?'

115

Nutmeg sobbed. 'No one knows we're here! We might NEVER get out!'

*           *           *

Tumtum, meanwhile, was pacing up and down the fish tank, thinking he might never escape either. The General and Nutmeg did not know he was here, so who would rescue him?

He gazed up at the glass walls in despair. He would have given anything to get out, but they were much too high for him to climb.

Soon it got very cold. The wind bit through the cracks in the shed wall, and the window was covered only with a flapping sheet of tarpaulin. Tumtum had no light to see by, so there was nothing to do but snuggle up in the sock and wait until morning. But he was much too worried to sleep. He lay gazing into the darkness, and thinking of Nutmeg, and of his warm bed at Nutmouse Hall.

Then suddenly, in the dead of night, he heard a noise.

Tumtum sat up in his sock in

surprise. It sounded like the patter of paws. And next moment he saw tiny flickers of light.

He slipped out of his sock and crept to the wall of the tank, rubbing away a little patch of dust with his paw so he could see out.

And when he peered down to the floor, he saw three black figures flashing torches. It was too dark to see their faces, but when they spoke he recognised their voices at once.

It was Goldfang and Snout and Punch! And then suddenly, in the flickering torchlight, Tumtum saw the toy helicopter, parked beside a flowerpot.

*So that's where they've been hiding it*, he thought in astonishment. *No wonder I couldn't see it under the sink—they've been keeping it in the shed! They must have flown in the window.*

Tumtum kept as still as stone. The mice did not know he was there, and he feared that if he made the slightest sound they might hear him. They were scurrying all round the floor, as if they were searching for something—and

Tumtum soon learned what it was.

'There's some!' Snout squealed, shining his torch on a ball of thick green twine. 'We can use this to pull the coins up from under the floorboards.'

'Good. Gnaw some off,' his father replied briskly. 'Then let's get back to Nutmouse Hall. I don't want to leave our prisoners unguarded.'

'Huh! I wouldn't worry about them,' Snout sniggered. 'That cellar door's made of solid tin; they'll never break out. Did you hear the General squealing through the keyhole after we locked them in? "Let me out! Do you know who I am?" What a twit.'

Tumtum was horrified. So they had broken into Nutmouse Hall, and locked Nutmeg and the General in the cellar. Nutmeg would be frightened out of her wits.

'I wonder what those kids did with Nutmouse,' Punch snarled. 'I 'ope they've put 'im somewhere 'e can't escape.'

'Wouldn't he howl if he could see us tomorrow night, flying off with a helicopter full of gold,' Snout gloated. 'Silly old fool. Fancy living at Nutmouse Hall all this time and never noticing there was a fortune hidden *right at the bottom of the stairs!* He must have run over that crooked floorboard a thousand times.'

The mice all cackled. 'Tonight, Operation Gold! Then tomorrow we shall be RICH!' Goldfang hissed.

*'Rich, rich, RICH!'* Snout cried, clapping his paws in delight. 'Rich as can be!' And soon they were all joining in, dancing in circles and hooting and shrieking with glee.

Tumtum watched them from the fish tank, his heart thumping. He knew exactly which floorboard Snout must be referring to. There was an uneven one lying just at the bottom of the stairs. He and Nutmeg had often clambered over it on their way to the attic. To think that there had been gold buried under it all this time!

But how could he stop Goldfang from stealing it? Somehow, he must get a message to Arthur and Lucy. They had promised to come back and feed him tomorrow morning—so that was his chance. But how could he communicate with them?

*They can't understand anything I say*, he thought despairingly. *And I can't write them a message, because I've no pen! Oh, if only I'd been wearing my other jacket.* Tumtum's fountain pen and his notebook were in the pocket of his corduroy jacket, which was the one he normally wore. But today he was wearing his tweed one, and the pockets were empty.

Presently, the three mice loaded their twine into the helicopter, and flew out through the window. Then Tumtum was alone again. But his mind was racing. All night long he paced about the fish tank, wondering what to do.

And as the night slipped by, his hopes started fading. But problems are sometimes easier to solve in the daylight. And when morning came, Tumtum had an idea.

# Chapter Thirteen

'That's it!' Tumtum cried, jumping from his sock in excitement. 'Oh, how clever! How brilliant! How witty, how wise!'

He ran to the wall of the fish tank, and gazed up at in delight. So what that he didn't have a pen and paper! He would write the children a message in the dust.

He dithered a moment, wondering what to say—but then he heard voices outside, as the children came running across the garden. So he hastily rolled up his sleeve, and scrawled out the first words that came to him:

You have caught the wrong mouse. Nutmeg is in danger. LET ME GO!

---

Tumtum wrote each word back to front, so that the children would be able to read it from the other side of the fish tank. And just as he was finishing, the shed door was flung open, and in they came.

Lucy was carrying Tumtum's breakfast—half an oatcake, and an egg cup full of milk. But when she saw the message written on the side of the tank, she dropped them in fright.

The children read it in astonishment. 'I told you he wasn't a bad mouse!' Lucy cried. 'But what could have happened to Nutmeg? Oh, come on Arthur, quick. We must let him go.'

But Arthur was looking at Tumtum suspiciously. 'He couldn't really have written that,' he said.

'But who else could have done it?' Lucy asked.

'I don't know. It must be some sort of trick,' Arthur said.

But then Tumtum settled the matter. While Arthur watched in amazement, he drew his paw through the dust once again, and signed his name with a flourish:

123

# Tumtum Nutmouse

'There!' Lucy said. 'What did I tell you?' She gently reached into the fish tank, and cupped her hand. Lucy had always been a little frightened of mice. But as Tumtum clambered up on to her palm, she felt no fear, just a slight tickle from his shoes.

'Where shall we put him?' Arthur said.

'Let's set him free in the kitchen— that's where we found him,' Lucy replied.

So they carried Tumtum back into Rose Cottage, and set him down on the kitchen floor. Tumtum was longing to get back to Nutmeg. But he did not dare run under the dresser while the children were watching, as it would give their hiding place away.

So he stood there impatiently, wishing they would disappear.

'We'd better get him something else to eat,' Arthur said. 'I'll find the other half of that biscuit.'

'And I'll get some more milk,' Lucy

said, turning to the fridge.

But when they looked back a moment later, Tumtum had gone.

*       *       *

Tumtum crouched under the dresser, peering through the broken gates at Nutmouse Hall. The lights were all lit, and he could see the bulldozer lying smashed into the front door. Then suddenly Goldfang appeared at the drawing room window. He stood there a while, staring into the dark, and Tumtum feared he had been seen. But presently Goldfang turned away, and sat down at the table.

Tumtum seized his chance, and quickly crept round to the side of the house to the little grated window that opened into the cellar. He crouched down to listen, but there was no sound coming from inside.

'Psssst!' he hissed. 'Nutmeg, General, are you there?'

There was no reply.

Tumtum felt a rush of fear, wondering what Goldfang and the

others had done to them.

'*Nutmeg, General*,' he tried again. '*It's me!*'

And then, to his joy, Nutmeg's tiny brown nose came twitching through the bars.

'Oh, Tumtum, thank goodness you've come,' she whimpered. 'I've been so worried about you. We didn't know where you'd been taken.'

'What took you so long, Nutmouse?' the General demanded impatiently, pushing up his nose beside her. 'We've been locked up in here a *whole* night! And all we've had to eat is a stale hazelnut.'

'I would have come sooner, but I've been locked up too,' Tumtum whispered. And Nutmeg and the General listened in astonishment as he hurriedly told them about his adventure in the garden shed, and how he had discovered where the gold was hidden.

'Oh, Tumtum, you are clever,' Nutmeg whispered. 'I thought we'd never find out where the coins were.'

'But how are we going to get to

127

them if we are locked up in here?' the General said. 'Can't you sneak inside the house, Nutmouse, and unlock the cellar door?'

'It's too dangerous,' Tumtum whispered. 'Goldfang's in the drawing room—I saw him in the window—and I don't know where the others are. If I tried to get inside, they'd be sure to see me. I shall have to wait in the Mildews' kitchen, then sneak back into Nutmouse Hall and let you out tonight, when they come out to steal the gold. But meanwhile I shall write a letter to Arthur and Lucy, explaining exactly where the coins are hidden, and telling them to fetch them at once. So Goldfang and his gang will be too late.'

'But how will the children lift up the floorboard?' Nutmeg asked anxiously. 'It's as thick as a tabletop, and it's nailed down. The children will need a pickaxe.'

'And if Goldfang and the others see what the children are up to, they'll dive under the floor and move the coins somewhere else, before the children can get to them,' the General added.

'It won't work, Nutmouse. We need a better plan.' And the General soon thought of one. 'Listen,' he whispered excitedly. 'Let's leave the crooks to carry on just as they intended. Let them sneak out tonight and drag all the coins up from under the floor, and load them into the helicopter—just as they'd planned. But meanwhile, Nutmouse, you must send Arthur and Lucy a letter, telling them to lie in wait on the upstairs landing. Ask them to keep very quiet, and wait until the very last coin has been loaded into the helicopter, and until all three mice have climbed into their seats. Then, just as they're about to fly away, the children can rush downstairs and catch them!'

Tumtum and Nutmeg thought it was a capital plan. 'It's brilliant!' Nutmeg whispered. 'Then Arthur and Lucy can get the gold *and* catch the thieves, all at the same time! Just think how excited they'll be!'

The General looked very smug. He felt in charge again, and he started conducting the operation from behind bars: 'Nutmouse, hurry to the attic and leave Arthur and Lucy their instructions,' he said bossily. 'Then you must hide in the Mildews' kitchen, and wait until Goldfang and the others come out. When they do, come straight back to Nutmouse Hall, and unlock the cellar door. Now hurry!'

Tumtum and Nutmeg nuzzled each other farewell through the grate. Then Tumtum tiptoed back around the side of the house, and crept out of the broom cupboard.

He intended to go straight to the attic. But when he poked his nose out from under the dresser, he pulled back in fright. Mr Mildew and the children were all in the kitchen!

Tumtum dared not go out now. He had taken a risk already, revealing his identity to the children. But he must never let them discover where he lived.

He waited nearly an hour until finally the children went into the garden, and he was able to sneak out while Mr Mildew was reading a newspaper.

He made straight for the children's room, hardly pausing for breath as he ran up the thick skirting beside the stairs, then crossed the landing and clambered up the steep wooden steps to the attic.

It was a long way for someone two inches tall, but Tumtum didn't stop. Finally, he heaved himself over the top step, then raced across the floor and dived into Lucy's satchel. He hauled a biro from her pencil case, and neatly nibbled a page from her spelling book. Then he dragged them both out on to the floor. And holding the pen in both arms—for it was a good deal taller than he was—he hastily scrawled out his orders:

*Dear Arthur and Lucy,*

*Three very bad mice have moved into Rose Cottage, and they are trying to do you all manner of harm. It was they who stole your toy helicopter, and broke into the doll's house, and ate your chocolates—and now they have taken Nutmeg prisoner!*
*But you can catch them, if you do exactly as I say. The mice have*

132

*discovered a secret horde of ancient gold coins, hidden under the hall floorboards! And they intend to steal them tonight!*

*They will creep out at midnight, and load the gold into the helicopter, then fly away. So you must lie in wait for them on the upstairs landing! But be patient. Wait until every last coin has been hauled up from under the floor, and loaded into the helicopter, and until all three mice have taken their seats in the cockpit, ready to take off ... and catch them as they try to escape!*

*Then the gold will be yours, and Nutmeg and I will be safe.*

*Love,*

*Tumtum.*

When he had finished, Tumtum rolled the letter into a cylinder, and swung it over his shoulder. And with a final burst of strength, he clambered up the covers on to Lucy's bed, and dropped it on her pillow.

# Chapter Fourteen

Tumtum hurried back to the kitchen and looked for somewhere to hide. He wanted to be within sight of the dresser, so that he could see when the Goldfangs and Punch came sneaking out. But they mustn't see him.

He spotted just the place.

*I shall hide in the vegetable rack*, he thought.

He ran across the floor and scrambled into it. Then he wriggled down inside a cabbage, pulling the soft green leaves all around him. Tumtum yawned. His trip to the attic had taken up the best part of the morning, and now it was nearly noon. But he was still in for a long wait, for the Goldfangs and Punch were not due to carry out their burglary until midnight. But Tumtum kept a close eye on the broom cupboard all the same, in case they came out sooner.

He could hear the children talking next door in the drawing room, and he

wished they would go upstairs and find his letter. Just think how excited they would be!

But then suddenly, at about one o'clock, Mr Mildew walked into the kitchen holding a canvas bag. 'Come on!' he shouted. 'We'll be late for the bus!'

A moment later, Arthur and Lucy came in, carrying rucksacks.

'We'll have to get a move on,' Mr Mildew said agitatedly. 'I promised Aunt Celia we'd be there by two.'

Tumtum watched in dismay as they all hurried outside, and slammed the door shut behind them. He and Nutmeg had often heard the children talk about their Great Aunt Celia, and he knew that she lived miles away— in another village! Mr Mildew and the children would be gone for ages. And why were they all carrying bags? *Perhaps they're going to spend the night*, he thought anxiously. *Then our whole plan will be in ruins!*

Tumtum dared not go back into the broom cupboard to tell Nutmeg and the General what had happened, in case one of the other mice saw him.

There was nothing to do but wait, and hope the children came back in time.

It was a miserable afternoon for Tumtum, crouching inside the cabbage, watching the garden door. The hours dragged by, and nothing happened at all. Teatime came and went, and he had not a scrap to eat. He was so hungry, he started nibbling on the rubbery leaves of his cabbage. Yuck! Tumtum liked cabbage when Nutmeg fried it with butter and bacon—but raw cabbage didn't taste nice at all.

Soon it got dark, and still there was no sign of the children.

*They must be spending the night,* Tumtum thought miserably, for it was well past supper time. *Now what are we going to do? I'll never be able to stop the Goldfangs and Punch on my own. I shall have to try and sneak back into the broom cupboard, and warn the General what's happened.*

And he was about to clamber down from the vegetable rack, when suddenly the garden door burst open, and the children and their father tramped back in.

Tumtum was very relieved. He peeked out of the cabbage, watching them silently. Mr Mildew went straight up to his study, but the children stayed in the kitchen to make some hot chocolate.

'What a long day!' Arthur yawned. 'I do like going to see Aunt Celia, but once she started telling all her war stories again, I thought we'd never get away.'

'I know,' Lucy said. 'We have heard them rather a lot of times. And then when she suggested we stay the night, I was frightened Dad would say yes, and we'd have had to sleep in that horrid spare room again. It's so full of cats' hairs, last time I spent a night in there, I went on sneezing for a whole week!'

'Yes, I'm glad he said we had to get back,' Arthur agreed. 'Come on, let's go upstairs, and see if anything else has been taken.'

'I hope not,' Lucy said. 'It's bad luck that we had to be out for the whole day, just when all these strange things are going on.'

Tumtum watched from his cabbage

as the children carried their mugs upstairs. He gave an exhausted sigh. Things might come right after all! If Arthur and Lucy hadn't come home, the whole plan would have failed. But now they would find his letter in good time—and when they learned that there was gold hidden under the floorboards, they were sure to do just as he said.

He looked at his watch, stifling a yawn. There were still three hours to go until midnight, and his eyelids were feeling very heavy.

Tumtum usually had a snooze after breakfast, and another snooze after lunch, and sometimes he even had a short snooze after his tea. But today he hadn't snoozed at all. He had been feeling too anxious. And when he thought of all the snoozes he had missed, he felt snoozier than ever.

He settled down deep in his cabbage, pulling the leaves tight round him to keep warm. It felt quite comfortable.

*Who would have thought a cabbage could be so cosy*, he thought. *I must recommend one to poor old Mr and Mrs*

*Churchmouse. They were telling me just the other day how they couldn't afford a proper bed—well, next I see them, I shall tell them to look out for a soft old cabbage instead.*

And as he snuggled down, Tumtum thought of all the other mice to whom he might recommend a cabbage for a bed. Poor Tommy Twigmouse ... and old Miss Tinkertail, who hadn't a cotton reel to her name ... and that young field mouse who slept in a draughty paper bag outside the village shop ... *Yes, yes, yes,* Tumtum thought sleepily. *I really must tell them all how comfortable a cabbage can be. And ... and ...'*

And *Zzzzzz!* Tumtum was fast asleep.

\*　　　\*　　　\*

The children, meanwhile, were very excited to find his letter on Lucy's pillow.

'Gold coins, buried under *our* floorboards!' Lucy gasped. 'Isn't it thrilling! Oh, I'm so glad we let Tumtum free!'

'What horrid mice they must be, to try and steal our gold, and to take Nutmeg prisoner,' Arthur remarked. 'We'd better make sure we catch them.'

He looked at his watch. 'Tumtum says they're planning to carry out the raid at midnight, which means we've got ages to wait. I hope we don't fall asleep and miss everything.'

'Oh, don't be daft,' Lucy said. 'Of course we won't fall asleep. How could we *possibly* fall asleep in the middle of an adventure like this. I shouldn't be able to sleep tonight however hard I tried.'

The children took as long as they could getting ready for bed, then they lay awake, talking excitedly. They heard the clock downstairs strike ten, then eleven . . . and at some point after that, Lucy gave a loud yawn. And as soon as Lucy started yawning, Arthur started too.

'Less than an hour to go now,' he said, pinching himself to stay awake.

'Well I hope you're not going to fall asleep,' Lucy said crossly.

'Of course I'm not,' Arthur replied.

'I'm just saying that it's less than an hour . . . less than an hour . . . *Zzzzzz!*'

First it was Tumtum, and now Arthur was asleep too!

Lucy sighed. Really, Arthur was being a baby. Fancy falling asleep when there was so much to look forward to. She lay in bed, trying to imagine what the gold coins would look like. Perhaps they would have engravings of Emperors on them, with crowns and long noses. And she wondered what the thieving mice looked like, and where Tumtum lived . . . and soon she had so many different thoughts spinning round her head that they all became a blur. And by the time the clock struck midnight, Lucy was asleep too.

# Chapter Fifteen

Tumtum was still slumbering peacefully in his cabbage, dreaming of Nutmeg and of Nutmouse Hall, and of porridge for breakfast and crumpets for tea, and of the toasty little fire in his library. He had an expression of deep contentment on his face.

But then something woke him. He sat up with a start, trying to think where he was. He was very stiff, and it was so dark, he could barely see his paws. And everything smelled of cabbage! Suddenly, he remembered the events of earlier that day. 'Oh, dear! I hope I haven't been asleep long!' He gulped.

Then there was a roar, and a blaze of lights—and when Tumtum peered out, he saw the toy helicopter flying over the kitchen table, towards the hall.

He waited until it had disappeared around the door, then he quickly clambered out of the vegetable rack, and raced across the kitchen to

Nutmouse Hall.

He went straight inside, picking his way over the splintered remains of his front door. Then he snatched the lantern from the hall table, and hurtled down the passage to the cellar. He swiftly drew the bolts, and pulled open the door—and when Nutmeg and the General saw him coming down the steps, they let out a loud cheer.

They had only been in the cellar since yesterday, but it felt like a whole month had passed. They were damp and shivering; and it had been torture to have to sit in the dark, not knowing what was happening in Nutmouse Hall.

'Oh, Tumtum! Thank goodness you've come!' Nutmeg cried, hobbling up to him on her stick.

'What's going on outside? Has the raid begun?' the General barked.

'Yes, they've just flown through to the hall,' Tumtum replied. 'I came as soon as I could.'

'Are the children on the landing?' the General demanded.

'I'm sure they are,' Tumtum said. 'I told them to be there by midnight, and I know they wouldn't be late for something as important as this.'

The General briskly rubbed the cobwebs off his jacket and started to look more as a General should. He was furious with Goldfang for getting the better of him last night, and he was longing for his revenge. 'Come on, let's go and watch the fun!' he cried.

Everyone wanted to see the mice being caught. But Nutmeg's leg was throbbing again, and Tumtum and the General had to help her up the steps. She was in too much pain to leave Nutmouse Hall.

'Don't worry about me,' she said firmly. 'You two go on—the children might need you. I'll stay here. I shall be quite safe now those brutes have gone.'

Tumtum did not like to leave Nutmeg behind. But she insisted he go with the General. So he helped her through to the drawing room, and tucked her back up on the sofa. Then he and the General crept out into the Mildews' kitchen.

It was very dark, but they could see the lights of the toy helicopter twinkling from the hall. They tiptoed across the room and peered round the door. The helicopter had just come down to land at the bottom of the stairs, but when Tumtum looked up at the landing, he gave a start: 'General, look!' he whispered. 'The children aren't there!'

The General was savage. 'How *dare* they disobey orders!' he spluttered. 'I'll go and shake them out of their beds!'

'Keep back! Goldfang will see you!' Tumtum hissed, grabbing him by the jacket. And he stopped him just in time, for next moment the helicopter door creaked open, and Goldfang and his accomplices slithered out.

Goldfang was carrying a lantern. He held it up as Punch pulled open the rear hatch of the helicopter, and dragged out a brown sack. Tumtum and the General peered at it, wondering what it was. And as Punch turned round, they saw that it had red letters written on the side.

'E . . . X . . . P . . . L . . . *Explosives*!' Tumtum whispered.

The General nodded grimly. 'It looks

like they're going to blow a hole in the floor,' he said.

The General had often used explosives in his army days. He was quite used to them. But Tumtum was not. He watched in horror as Punch dragged the sack across the floor, until it was lying just by the edge of the crooked floorboard at the bottom of the stairs. Then Goldfang lit a match from his pocket, and tossed it down.

The three mice hurtled away, diving for cover under the umbrella rack. A moment later there was a deafening blast—*BAM!*—and a mass of tiny sparks shot up into the air.

Tumtum and the General crouched behind the door, clutching their heads in their paws. The noise echoed all round the hall. Then everything was very quiet.

'S-surely the children would have heard that?' Tumtum stammered. But it had only been a mouse-sized explosion. To a human ear, it would have sounded no louder than a saucer dropping to the floor.

Tumtum and the General watched

anxiously as the three mice crept back across the hall, and inspected the bomb damage with their lantern. The blast had made a small, round hole, a couple of centimetres wide—just big enough for a mouse to wriggle through.

Snout ran to the helicopter and fetched the green twine. Then, holding one end himself, and passing the other end to Punch, he held his stomach in tight, and squeezed down through the hole in the floor.

Punch and Goldfang peered after him.

'Hurry,' Goldfang barked. 'We haven't got all night.'

Ten seconds passed. Then twenty. And finally, from under the floorboards, there came a muffled shout: 'PUUUUUULLLLLLLL!'

Punch gripped the twine with both paws and, bracing his legs on the floor, pulled until the sweat poured down his nose. Tumtum and the General watched in astonishment. Punch was a strong mouse, but his face was purple with strain.

'One coin couldn't be as heavy as

that,' Tumtum whispered. 'He must be pulling up the whole bag.'

But then Punch let out an agonised grunt, and gave the twine a final, gut-busting wrench—and up came the biggest, most magnificent gold coin that Tumtum and the General had ever seen.

It was as tall as a mouse—and thicker than cardboard. And despite all its years of dust and neglect, the gold still gleamed so brightly it made them squint.

Tumtum and the General watched in amazement as Punch let the coin clang to the floor. Then the twine was tossed back down to Snout, and a few moments later another cry of 'PUUUULLLLL!' rang up from down below.

The process began again, until finally up came a second coin, as dazzling as the first. Then a third coin appeared . . . and a fourth . . . and a fifth . . . until at last there were a dozen gold coins heaped on the hall floor.

'That's the lot! Get me up!' Snout squealed. Punch hauled him up, and

151

the three mice started wheeling the coins to the helicopter and heaving them into the hatch.

Tumtum and the General were getting very jittery, for still there was no sign of Arthur and Lucy. Soon all but one of the coins had been loaded into the helicopter, ready for take-off. Another few seconds and the thieves would be on their way.

'Oh, BLAST those children,' the General fumed. 'WHERE ARE THEY?'

But just when everything seemed lost, there was a creak upstairs on the landing.

# Chapter Sixteen

Lucy had been having a very strange dream. She    thought she was being chased up the cottage stairs by a huge white mouse—but just as it was about to catch up with her, she heard something crash.

She sat up in bed with a start. And when she looked at her clock she gulped. It was after midnight!

'Arthur,   quick,   wake   up!'   she whispered. 'They'll have got away!'

She leaned over Arthur's bed and shook him. He sat up blearily. But when he remembered about the mice, he jumped out of bed at once.

The children did not dare turn on the lights in case they frightened them away. So they groped their way down to the landing in the dark.

Tumtum and the General were still crouched under the kitchen door. And when they saw the children they gave a silent cheer. 'I told you they wouldn't let   us   down,'   Tumtum   whispered proudly—but Lucy felt certain they would be too late.

Oh, how could we have been so stupid, falling asleep like that! she thought furiously.

But when they peered down to the hall, they saw the most astonishing sight. The toy helicopter was parked at the bottom of the stairs, with its headlights twinkling. And there were three mice standing next to it, all dressed in black. One was holding up a lantern, and the other two were heaving something into the helicopter's hatch.

The children could not see what the object was, but it was clearly very heavy. The mice were bent double, stooping under its weight. Finally, they managed to push it inside. Then all three quickly climbed into the cockpit. The helicopter's engine growled, and the propellers started to spin.

'Quick!' Lucy cried. 'Catch them!'

Tumtum and the General watched in trembling excitement as the children ran down the stairs.

'Hurry!' the General cried. 'Don't

let them escape!' He could not bear to be excluded from the action, and ran out from under the door, barking encouragement—

But the children's eyes were fixed on the helicopter.

Arthur was in front of Lucy, but as he reached the bottom step the helicopter span up into the air. He grabbed at it, but it was out of reach, flying almost as high as the ceiling. Lucy scrambled on to the chest, trying to catch it—but it was too quick for her, swiftly turning and buzzing into the kitchen.

The children ran after it, jumping up and trying to pull it from the air. When Lucy turned on the kitchen light, they could see the three mice jeering down at them from the cockpit.

The mood inside the helicopter was very jaunty, for the thieving mice were almost free! They were but inches away from the open window, and once they had flown through it, there would be no stopping them.

'Ha! Ha!' Goldfang shrieked. 'The gold is *OURS!'*

'OURS!' they all cried.

But the toy helicopter was showing signs of strain. The gold was too heavy for it, and the propellers had started to hiccup. Tumtum and the General peered up at it in suspense. 'It's going to crash!' the General cried gleefully.

And suddenly the engine spluttered and gave a belch—and all at once the helicopter tipped down its nose, and plummeted into the sink.

*BOMPF!*

It landed in a dirty frying pan, splattering head first into the oil. The engine thudded to a stop, and a thin feather of peaty black smoke billowed from the cockpit. Then the door creaked open, and the three mice staggered out. When they saw the children peering down at them, their eyes blackened with rage.

'How *dare you* provide us with a faulty helicopter! You'll pay for this!' Goldfang shouted.

'We'll tear your school books to shreds, and burn down the doll's house!' Punch snarled.

'I'll fill your pencil cases with mouse

156

droppings!' Snout cried, stamping his fat little paws.

But all Arthur and Lucy could hear was a chorus of nasty squeals.

They stared at the furious little creatures in astonishment. 'Look,' Arthur said, pointing at the Goldfangs. 'Those two have got gold teeth.'

The children had seen mice wearing clothes before, but they had never seen ones with gold teeth, so they were very surprised. 'It must be a rare breed,' Lucy said.

'Come on, let's see if the coins are inside the helicopter,' Arthur said excitedly. But the children hesitated to reach into the sink, for the mice looked as if they might bite them.

So Arthur took a scrubbing brush from the draining board, and drove the mice into the corner while Lucy quickly snatched the helicopter out.

'Give that back!' Goldfang screeched, waving his fist. And he called the children all sorts of names, which it is just as well they couldn't hear.

Tumtum and the General watched

from the doorway as Arthur and Lucy emptied the coins out on to the kitchen table and pored over them. They were huge, and clearly very old. The edges were worn down, and they were covered in strange symbols.

'I wonder what they are,' Arthur said. 'I bet Dad will know. Do you think we should go and wake him up?'

But Mr Mildew had been woken already by all the clattering in the kitchen, and he came stumbling downstairs in his dressing gown.

He was not at all pleased to find the children up. 'What on earth are you doing? It's the middle of the night,' he said crossly. But when he saw the gold coins lying on the table, he went very quiet.

He sat down silently at the table, turning them over and over in his hands. His jaw was gaping, and his eyes had started to gleam.

'Are they—are they valuable?' Arthur asked hesitantly.

'*Valuable?* Why, these coins are worth a small fortune!' Mr Mildew cried. 'Don't you see, my dears! They'll solve all our woes! We'll have enough money to pay the gas bill, and the electricity bill, and the water bill, and the telephone bill! We'll be able to mend the window ... and repair the roof ... We won't have to sell Rose Cottage after all! Oh, how I'd been *praying* they'd turn up!'

'*Turn up?*' Lucy asked. 'But ... I thought ... Do you mean you've seen these coins before?'

'Well, of course!' Mr Mildew cried. 'They belonged to my father, and he gave them to me years ago, when I first moved in here. I knew they were very rare, and I was so frightened I'd lose them, I hid them away ... and then a month passed, and I couldn't remember where I'd put them. I turned the whole house upside down, but they'd gone. I assumed they must have been stolen. Wherever did you find them?'

'They were under that wonky floorboard in the hall,' Lucy said.

'The hall! Why, of course! *That's* where I put them!' Mr Mildew exclaimed, slapping a hand to his forehead. 'Oh, how stupid of me to forget! How mad, how scatty, how . . . how . . . But hang on a minute,' he said suddenly. 'How did you find them there?'

'Well,' Lucy began, 'we'd never have found them if it wasn't for the mice—'

'Mice?' Mr Mildew asked, looking baffled.

'That's right,' Lucy said. 'We caught them just a few minutes ago. They pulled the coins up from under the floor with a piece of string, then they loaded them into the toy helicopter, and they were going to fly away of course, but luckily for us the helicopter crashed.'

Mr Mildew looked very bewildered. He was only a grown-up, and it was all a bit much for him to take in. But then suddenly there was a loud squeal from the sink. 'What was that?' he asked, sitting up with a jolt.

And when the children showed him their prisoners, he was quite amazed. He took off his glasses, and gave them a good polish. He had seen some strange mice before at Rose Cottage—

but none like these. 'Gold teeth,' he muttered. 'Well, well, well. Well, well, well, well, well.'

'What shall we do with them?' Lucy said. 'I'm not sure I want to keep them. But we can't just let them go, not after all the trouble they've caused.'

'Certainly not!' their father said. 'How many mice have you seen with gold teeth? These revolting creatures deserve a wider audience. I shall call the pet shop first thing in the morning, and ask them to come and fetch them. They won't have seen a breed like this before. I should think they'll fetch a very high price.'

Tumtum and the General nodded their approval. 'Hah! That will serve them right!' the General humphed.

Arthur and Lucy thought it was a splendid idea too.

But when the prisoners heard their fate they let out a howl of protest. 'A pet shop! *How dare you send us to a pet shop!*' Goldfang roared. 'We're not *pets*. We're criminals!'

It was a horrid, whiny noise. 'I don't think we should leave them in the sink overnight,' Lucy said, wrinkling her nose. 'It's not very deep. They might climb out. And what if we want a drink of water?'

'Where shall we put them?' Mr Mildew asked.

'I know,' Arthur said. 'Let's put them in the fish tank. They won't escape from that.'

At the news that they were to be imprisoned in a fish tank, the mice let out an even louder protest. Punch picked up a dirty teaspoon, and started bashing it furiously against the side of the sink.

'What a din they make,' Mr Mildew said, covering his ears.

'What shall we carry them in?' Lucy asked.

'Saucepans,' Mr Mildew suggested. But it was not at all easy: Mr Mildew caught Snout first, pushing him into the first saucepan with a wooden spoon; then Arthur rounded up Punch with a soup ladle; and finally Lucy caught Goldfang, scooping him into a casserole dish.

Then Mr Mildew took the torch,

and they carried their prisoners out to the shed, and tipped them into the tank. The sock which had served as Tumtum's bed was still there, and there were some crumbs left in the saucer. But the mice were not at all happy.

'You brutes! You'll pay for this!' Goldfang roared, shaking his fist in a fury.

'We'll eat you alive!' Punch squealed feebly.

The Mildews peered down at them in the torchlight, thinking what strange mice they were. 'Do you really think the pet shop will take them?' Lucy asked. 'I know they're a rare breed. But they're so ugly, I wonder if anyone will want to buy them.'

'Of course they will,' Mr Mildew said. 'I told you, they'll be stars!'

Even so, neither Mr Mildew nor the children wanted to look at them much longer. So soon they went back inside. But they were too excited to go back to bed. Instead they sat up talking in the kitchen. Mr Mildew told the children that he had had the coins valued by an expert a long time ago, before he hid

them under the hall floor. And they had been worth a lot then—so now they would be worth even more.

'Will we be rich?' Arthur asked anxiously. He wasn't sure he liked the idea very much. Rich people lived in big houses—so he wondered if they would have to leave Rose Cottage after all, and move somewhere grander.

'Rich? Oh, gracious no!' Mr Mildew laughed. 'We won't be rich—no such luck. We just won't be quite so poor any more. And when I've paid off all my bills, there might be enough money to go on holiday. Somewhere far away,' he went on dreamily. '. . . India, or Africa, or South America . . . or Scotland perhaps!'

Mr Mildew had never taken Arthur and Lucy on holiday before, and they both thought it was a splendid plan. When they finally climbed upstairs to bed, their heads were swimming.

What a wonderful adventure it had been—and thanks to Tumtum, everything had worked out just right!

'There's something funny about Rose Cottage isn't there?' Arthur said.

'I mean, no one I know has mice like ours.'

'Something very funny,' Lucy agreed. She looked thoughtful. Then: 'Do you suppose Nutmeg might be a mouse?' she asked suddenly.

'I shouldn't think so,' Arthur replied. 'I mean, if she is a mouse, then why didn't she tell us?'

'Hmmm, I suppose it would be odd of her not to mention it,' Lucy agreed. 'I just thought ... well, seeing as she's such good friends with Tumtum, and he's a mouse ... But I suppose that doesn't prove anything. Oh, Arthur, do you think we'll ever find out who she really is?'

'I'm sure we will some day.' Arthur yawned.

But for the moment Nutmeg was hidden away in Nutmouse Hall, well out of sight.

Tumtum and the General had come home, and were busy telling her everything that had happened.

'Just think of it, dear! Mr Mildew hid the coins away, then forgot where he had put them!' Tumtum sighed. 'What an extraordinary man he is! But he said they really are rather valuable. So now he won't have to sell Rose Cottage after all!'

'Oh, Tumtum, isn't it wonderful!' Nutmeg cried. 'You must go up to the attic tonight and leave the children another letter, telling them where all the doll's house furniture is hidden.'

'Yes, of course,' Tumtum said. 'They were so excited about the coins they didn't mention the furniture again. But Lucy will be very pleased to get it back. Won't she be astonished when she looks under the sink, and finds that stinking bleach bottle!'

They all laughed. No one was in the mood for sleep, and they were all very hungry. So Tumtum scurried off to the kitchen, and laid a tray with scones and tea. Then he carried it back to the drawing room, and they sat up talking long into the night.

The General knew that Mrs Marchmouse would be worrying about him, so he planned to set off home as soon as it grew light. 'I shall call *The Mouse Times* tomorrow, and tell them what a hero I've been,' he said boastfully. 'How they'll cheer when they hear that I single-handedly caught three thieves riding in a stolen helicopter, and found a horde of buried treasure!

The General had forgotten that anyone else had played a part in the adventure—and Tumtum and Nutmeg hadn't the heart to remind him.

'I shall have to start tidying up in the morning,' Tumtum yawned. 'Those rascals have made a terrible mess of Nutmouse Hall. We'll need a new front door, and new gates too by the look of things. And I'm afraid you'll get a dreadful fright when you see the kitchen, dear. They've turned everything upside down.'

But Nutmeg didn't care. She was just glad that everyone was safe and well. 'I'll sort it all out when my leg's better,' she said. 'Goodness, what an adventure it's been! We seem to have so many of them—I hope we don't have any more.'

'Oh, I'm sure we won't,' Tumtum said confidently—but then Nutmeg remembered something he had told her earlier, and she started to frown.

'What is it, dear?' Tumtum asked.

'Oh, well ... it's nothing really,' Nutmeg said. 'It's just ... oh, Tumtum! You don't really think Mr Mildew will take the children on a *holiday*, do you? It sounds terribly dangerous. And you said he threatened to go somewhere *far away*.' Nutmeg had a sudden vision of Arthur and Lucy stranded in a desert, or sailing across an endless ocean, and she did not like the thought of it at all.

But Tumtum just laughed. 'Oh, you mustn't worry about that, dear—I shouldn't even have mentioned it. You know what Mr Mildew's like. He can hardly find his way to the village shop! Can you imagine him taking Arthur and Lucy on holiday? He'll never do it—you can be quite sure.'

Well I'm afraid he did. But that's another story.